NO PARADISO

WILLIAM WALL

BRANDON

A Brandon Original Paperback

First published in 2006 by Brandon
an imprint of Mount Eagle Publications
Dingle, Co. Kerry, Ireland, and
Unit 3, Olympia Trading Estate, Coburg Road, London N22 6TZ, England

www.brandonbooks.com

ISBN 0 86322 355 9

2 4 6 8 10 9 7 5 3 1

Mount Eagle Publications/Sliabh an Fhiolair Teoranta receives support from
the Arts Council/An Chomhairle Ealaíon.

Cover design: Anú Design
Typesetting by Red Barn Publishing, Skeagh, Skibbereen
Printed in the UK

Contents

for Liz

CONTRACTA PISCES ÆQUORA SENTIUNT

IACTIS IN ALTUM MOLIBUS

The fish senses the shrinking of the ocean
when he is thrown against the pier.

Horace, *Odes* III.1

In Xanadu

We slept fitfully then, uncertain of the slipshod hills of winking streets and bloody crosses, the streams that wound through everything, throwing that uncertain light in the eyes, on the buildings, as far as the sky even. And when we did not sleep, we lived along the streets, in the bars, in the groves of the college. Staying awake was not difficult. There were nightclubs, dances, flats and bedsits, even glorious starry winter nights. There was walking the hills where the streets wound in and out like water. And there was talk. Everyone talked about music; some talked philosophy or poetry or science. All of it, once the light was gone, in the grey pain of the next day, seemed utterly banal, utterly false. But we were convinced that memory played tricks. We were convinced that no one remembered exactly what had happened. That we had said things that surprised even ourselves with their beauty, ideas that ravished like Cinderellas but which had now fled without leaving even a slipper, or had unaccountably transformed themselves into ugly sisters.

It all changed when Nuala died. It was during our last term, just before exams. She was coming up to college from her sister's house, where baby number four had just been christened, when an articulated lorry pulled out across the road. The Mini was too big to slip underneath, and when the roof came off it took the top of Nuala's head with it.

Even though there are no endings really, even though each story is a continuum out of which we pluck what we call stories, which our own skill tricks us into thinking complete and self-sufficient, even though there is only one full stop, nevertheless, that death was a terminus at which all of us stopped and from which we set out again later in different directions. We never looked back.

I met Kevin as I climbed up the hill from Gaol Gate. He was sitting propped against the steel bars of the college, his coat raised around his ears, his head hanging. I could see, even before I recognised him, that he was drunk.

'Did you hear what I did?' He was looking up at me. I wondered if he could see who I was.

'Kevin.'

'Jesus, man,' he said. I helped him up and he leaned heavily on me. Where was he going?

'Man,' he said. 'I haven't a fucking clue. Know what I mean? Your place or mine?'

He laughed loudly and repeated it several times. 'Your place or mine?'

It wasn't far to my flat. On the way he argued with me about directions, insisting that I lived somewhere else. As we passed a garden with blackened hydrangeas bulging out through the fence, he leaned over and vomited noisily. When that was finished, he threw his head back and said, 'That's better anyway. I felt I had to get that off my chest. You know what they say . . . Drink it down, it'll do you good, and get it up, you'll feel better.'

'You said you were after doing something.'

'Shit. Don't remind me.'

He got up again and we struggled on. As we walked he told me.

'It was Dawkins's lecture. You know. The influence of *Beowulf* on Einstein's Theory of Relativity or something. Jesus, I hate Anglo-Saxon. Anyway, he started off with the slides again. The whole place in darkness at the flick of a switch. Presto, like. A moment of awed silence. Then – *the Ruthwell Cross.*'

'What else?'

'Every bloody lecture has a slide show, and every slide show starts off with the Ruthwell Cross. Anyway, the spirit moved me for once. As soon as I saw the Ruthwell Cross, and all the nuns with their pens poised, I couldn't stand it any more. So I shouted, I quote, *an obscenity* at the darkness. Only Dawkins was standing just behind me with the fucking remote control button.'

'What obscenity?'

'Ah, I just said *fuck the Ruthwell Cross* or words to that effect.'

'What did he say?'

'He threw me out. Blasphemy et cetera. The nuns were very upset apparently and were demanding an apology.'

'Did he say that?'

'Or words to that effect.'

'What did you say?'

He went through an elaborate, comical routine in which he pointed at himself and mouthed the words, *Who? Me?* His face all injured innocence. Then he joined his hands in front and spoke in a soft, even voice.

'I said the nuns were entitled to be upset. I said it was a despicable thing to do, but that I was under a lot of strain at the moment, and I hoped they would accept my apology in the spirit in which it was intended.'

'So?'

'So I'm only barred until next week. The nuns took a maternal interest in me and recommended a good prayer group, so I went off and got pissed out of my mind.'

'A perfectly natural reaction.'

By now we had reached my flat. He threw himself down on the couch and began to snore almost immediately. I went to bed myself. In those days my sleep was untroubled, and I slept until the alarm. Before I left to go over to a lecture, I looked in and saw that he was sleeping like a baby. The flat reeked of stale beer and other people's clothes.

Later he was awake. I fried sausages and eggs and bread, and we ate it listening to the one o'clock news. The price of beef, I remember, was going through the floor. Now I cannot remember why, but I remember we smiled knowingly – beef is not going to go through the floor around here, we were saying, students do not come in for such luxuries. We spoke for some time about food. Eventually Kevin asked me if I knew Nuala. But everybody knew Nuala. He said he had a date with her and did I think she'd go far?

Everyone knew Nuala was easy. She would sleep anywhere for anything. There were dozens of people who boasted of having slept with her.

'The best thing about Nuala,' he told me, 'is she has a car.'

Then we spoke about campus politics. We were agreed that the new union president was a cretin. His campaign had been one of carefully printed literature and well-organised public meetings. He was Ógra Fianna Fáil. Trust FF to organise it down to the last detail. We had distributed carelessly typed pamphlets for a left-wing candidate who had secured about 6 per cent of the vote, but retained the undying respect of the student body.

'So when are you meeting Nuala?' I asked.

'In about an hour. Here.'

'Here? How does she know you're here? Jesus. You were waiting for me last night.'

He grinned.

'Well,' he said, 'I could also fall asleep on the road. I did it before. If you didn't come along.'

He had cleared the table and aired the room, and generally made himself useful around, so I didn't object. Now, while I transcribed notes I had borrowed, he washed the ware. The clatter of dishes and the smell of soapy water reminded me of home. I could almost sense my mother standing behind me, facing out through the deep windows at the snowdrops, or the geraniums she husbanded through the winter.

Soon Nuala came. She was one of the college beauties, with an unusual face that looked dull in repose but was attractively mobile. When she smiled, it seemed to go into shards, like glass or facets of a kaleidoscope. She had a raucous voice and a fund of obscene stories. They left together in her car, and after they were gone I settled down to serious study.

When they came back, I heard their voices calling me through the letterbox. They were outside in the rain, and I could hear the engine of the car running and wipers dragging across the screen. I wanted to pretend I had heard nothing, but they just kept calling, so in the end I let them in to drip around the floors. Nuala switched off the engine and left the car parked where it was, half in, half out of the road. They were both drunk, and possibly high as well, and in high spirits. They had brought a six-pack and a bottle of cheap wine with them – Hirondelle I remember it was called – a two-litre bottle. Nuala told jokes and recited, verbatim, snatches from *Annie Hall*. Kevin recited a poem. We put on Leonard Cohen and listened while we drank. Nuala said 'Chelsea Hotel' always reminded her of herself. The bit about getting away and talking so wild and so free. She said she felt she talked too much and we both said no, that it was great to meet someone who talked as much as ourselves. So then she stood up and sang 'Chelsea Hotel No. 2', standing with her hands by her sides and her head thrown back in the attitude of a folksinger. She sang it like a ballad, a song of bitterness and pain, a little too fast maybe, but raw and intense. When she was finished, she slid in beside the table and drank what was left in her glass with a flourish, but we didn't feel like clapping. For a time we could think of nothing to say.

Nuala began to cry quietly, cradling the glass in two hands. She said we were nice boys, and why was it that she couldn't always go out with nice boys. Kevin said he wasn't sure he liked the idea.

Then they danced for a while and I sat on the floor. My head was swimming, but I was aware that something was out of control, like the governor had failed on some rickety machine. She was frightening and loveable, fragile and dangerous. She was intoxicating.

I stayed on the floor when Nuala and Kevin moved to the couch. I think I may have passed out or drifted into sleep, because when I woke up they were making love. I sat there for a moment watching them, mind clarified by unconsciousness, and saw the languid movements that are the language of the body, the small silent lock that a man and a woman turn, that brings intimacy and pain, safety and rejection. It seemed to me for an instant that I was watching the coupling of mythical creatures – a Paris and Helen, a Deirdre and Naoise. Then the mood passed and I felt the sour wine on my tongue, acid tumbling in my gut. It was five o'clock on a winter's morning and I was cold.

I got up and opened the curtains, and the lights had gone out all over the city. Houses were shut down. Nothing moved except the couple on the couch behind me in their own lightless circle. I left quietly and went to bed. Later I heard Kevin in the toilet, and later still I heard Nuala singing in the kitchen. I remember thinking they were here to stay and I would have to make sure my landlord didn't find out. Thinking of my landlord, I drifted into an uneven sleep, in which I returned periodically to near waking to hear the strange sound of someone else's morning.

But Nuala and Kevin never really moved in. Every morning they made plans about where they would go to next. The fact was Kevin had no place of his own. He simply hadn't bothered to look when the rush of advertisements came out in September. He had drifted from friend to friend since then, kipping on floors and armchairs, sustained by late nights and beer. Now, instead of Kevin actually moving in, his belongings began to accrue, each day bringing something forwarded from another doss. The last to come were books – scattered, lent, forgotten. The hated *Beowulf, King Lear,* Coleridge's poems, Berryman and Roethke, Mac Diarmaid. Abused prodigals, they took their places and were as unassuming as they could be while at the same time exuding an impression of permanence. When the books arrived, I knew I was stuck with Kevin. For a vagrant, he surprised me by the extent of his baggage. Nuala, on the other hand, had nothing to impede her, as if anything heavier than a change of clothes would have fatally burdened the red Mini.

Most of the time they were useful. Kevin cooked well. Nuala was fanatically clean. Sometimes I arrived home to find they had prepared something exotic like chicken Tandoori, cooked with real turmeric and cumin, or some exotic pastry that hadn't quite turned into what it should have been. Smells filled the flat, the hissing of pots, the burnt smell of spillages. On one occasion all three of us wrote an essay I had to hand in the following day.

What I found difficult to bear was the way their intimacy took control of the place. It was everywhere: Nuala's pants hanging out to dry, underclothes lying on chairs, toothbrushes, hairs on the furniture, notes. Even worse because less tangible was the air that filled every corner. I began to feel as if I were living their lives, as if I were an element in their complexity, a temporarily unused organ. The time would come when I would be again called upon to respond autonomously to stimuli, when expected reactions would be demanded of me. In the meantime, I must agree to be tended and ignored.

One day I came in from a walk along the river and knew immediately that something was happening. The door to the living room was ajar, and through the opening I could see that they were on the couch. I went straight into the kitchen. As soon as he heard me, Kevin came out. He was wearing a vest and shorts. One sock was still on.

'Hi. You're back.'

I said I hoped I wasn't intruding.

'Jesus, man, it's all over now. Are you making tea? Bring us in a cup when it's made, will you.'

'Fuck off,' I said. But I made the tea anyway.

They sat up when I came in. They were careless of their nakedness in a way I had never seen before I met them. Nuala was naked but had covered herself with his army-surplus jacket. I could see a single white breast, banded above and below by a faint suntan. As she moved her hand to take the tea, the skin stretched and softened, and the nipple quivered when she moved. Kevin stroked her arm as we spoke.

'We've something to say, man,' Kevin said.

Nuala giggled. 'I'm not pregnant or anything.'

'You're getting engaged,' I said. 'It'll be in *The Irish Times* and it'll be a long engagement until Kevin can get a job to support you.' It was a joke but they didn't laugh. 'All right,' I said, 'you've decided to go steady. He's giving you his fraternity pin.'

This time they laughed. Nuala said, 'He's giving me his pin

all right.' Then Kevin looked sheepish and Nuala poked him obviously in the ribs. He spoke slowly and carefully in the way they must have planned.

'Look,' he said, 'Jesus, I mean here we are, right? Living in your flat. I mean, it's generous, you know. Above and beyond the call of duty. You don't owe us anything. So, Nuala was saying – we were both thinking – that we ought to split the rent. Three ways, fair enough. And we owe you a few weeks. No bull, three ways exactly. Nuala has the waitress job, and I have the grant. What about that?'

I didn't want to say I would prefer if they left, because I knew they would, leaving an irreparable gash in the fabric of my days. But I knew if I let them pay I would be stuck with them. I said I couldn't possibly let them pay anything. They argued a bit, then suddenly they caved in, and Nuala reached forward and grabbed me by the head with both hands, both breasts coming clear of the fabric and tilting forwards and downwards. Tears swelled in her eyes.

'You're just beautiful,' she said. 'You're so beautiful.' She dragged me against her and I felt the warmth of those breasts and the smell of bodies and lovemaking. She said, 'We have a surprise. We're planning a trip and we want you to come along.'

'A trip?'

Kevin said, 'We're going to drive down to Dingle. Stay in a place down there for a couple of days and drink ourselves blind. Talk Irish and all that meaningful bullshit. Nuala is doing Irish.'

'Where are we going to get the money?'

They laughed.

'That's what we're telling you: we have the money. The grant, right? And Nuala has her job. It'll be incredible.'

It was settled. We were all going to Dingle as soon as it could be organised.

That night there was a party to celebrate the decision. They went around the college all day announcing the trip. The story was fantastic enough to attract hangers-on. I caught up with them at half-past ten in Starry's and was given a small whiskey and a pint of Carling. A medical student I knew was singing 'Peggy Gordon' in the style of The Dubliners, including the Dublin accent, and Nuala, fully clothed now, Indian style, with beads and bracelets, was listening intently, her mouth slightly open, a pink tip of tongue between her teeth. Kevin was arguing at the bar, with pursed, frustrated gestures. I was stopped as I went to find a stool by James Keane, a young poet. Almost incoherent with drink, he accused me of being bourgeois and soulless. I conceded gracefully and tried to move on.

Charlie Kennedy, one of the department tutors, an MA student, was kicking me in the ankle as I stood there, so I left the poet and sat beside him.

'That was an awful fucking essay you gave me,' he said. I could have done without that.

I didn't tell him it was a three-way production. I explained that I was caught for time, and that having Nuala and Kevin staying with me was an exhausting trip. He winked suggestively and said, 'I'd say you wouldn't get a wink of sleep with those fuckers, hah? At it all night. Nuala is fine half.' He glanced over his shoulder repeatedly and was bent down in a conspiratorial crouch.

'A whatayacallit *ménage à trois*. Fuckin hell.' And he groaned suggestively.

Now that Nuala and Kevin had become long term, I was surprised by the number of people who hadn't slept with her. It was as if the relationship that had developed had called their bluff. Not that anyone came up to me and said, 'Hey, I never slept with Nuala, I was only joking.' It was obvious enough, though, in the way they spoke about her. Charlie Kennedy, for example, had once boasted to me that he had screwed her three times in one night on the back seat of her Mini. I remembered that, because I remembered asking whether it was possible to make love in the back seat of a Mini, and he had made the same wink and said something about the Kama Sutra and acrobats.

Somebody had a guitar, and in the public bar a box player was found who, for a tray of Guinness, played until closing time. When we were put out, I told them to follow the crowd to my place.

A lot of people were dancing in the living room and the air was heavy with smoke. In the bedroom, people were sitting around drinking quietly. Here and there a couple grappled desultorily. It was in the kitchen that the serious drinking was happening. The six-packs and wine bottles were ranged on the counter, and the sink was full of empties and caps. A confused Charlie Kennedy was jammed against the sink by a dark-haired woman who kept saying he was invading her personal space. The medical student, who was drunk and surprised to find himself at a party where he knew nobody, was singing snatches of 'Raglan Road'. The guitarist was sitting cross-legged on the kitchen table, apparently taking up little space, and picking out the notes of a tune the box player was giving him.

I was looking for Nuala and Kevin but couldn't find them. Instead I found a girl I knew sitting on the end of the stairs drinking from the neck of a bottle of Paddy.

'I'm going to kill myself,' she told me, matter-of-factly. 'Course, it's a cry for help. I wouldn't do it if I didn't need help.'

I said, 'If you kill yourself here it'll be embarrassing.'

She looked at me blankly.

'I'll have to explain to the landlord how I found a girl on the premises who isn't mentioned in the letting agreement.'

'Fuck off,' she said, and went back to drinking.

I sat down beside her, and after a time she passed me the bottle.

'Do I know you?' she asked.

'This is my flat.'

'Oh Jesus, sorry.'

I named a few people she might know and told her who I was, as clearly as I could manage. I was surprised how much I was defined by my friends. 'You're OK,' she said. 'Anybody who knows my friends knows me.'

Her name was Terry Kane.

'Want to dance?'

She smiled crookedly and winked.

'Fucking drink,' she said. 'No good.'

She got up and walked unsteadily ahead of me into the living room. When we began to dance, she wrapped her arms tightly around my neck and put her head on my shoulder. I put my hands on her back, inside her shirt, and we danced like that for a time. Then we went into the bedroom and sat in a corner. There were fewer people there now, and somebody had made a joint. It passed slowly from finger to finger, and when it shrank it was held on a pin. It was wasted out before it reached us, so another was rolled. I pulled deeply, holding my breath, and heard the ritual quiet bells. Blindly I passed it on, but she didn't smoke. Instead it began its passage once more, a glowing tip circling like a rosary, until it expended itself in warmth.

The conversation was haphazard.

'Oh, great hit,' someone said and some people laughed tenderly.

James Keane, the poet, declared that Dylan had betrayed us. The revolution, he said, could do without Dylan. Terry began to sing 'It Ain't Me Babe' and everyone listened intently. After two verses she stopped.

'I don't smoke shit,' she said, 'because I like to keep a clear head on me. Shit only screws you up.'

'Oh no,' I said, 'you have it all wrong. It's the other way round.'

A chorus approved me. We were all upset.

'No,' Terry said. 'It's always the same. Anyway, if you're going to smoke you have to be happy, right?' Everyone nodded. I could hear the movement in the darkness.

'Well, I'm not happy. How could I be happy? I'm going to fail my finals. Right? My dad'll beat the shite out of me. I'll be destroyed. My best friend split with me last night. I mean, I'm totally fucked up, right? That's it.'

'Hey,' somebody said, 'there's a law. Your old fella can't beat you.'

Someone else said, 'So why don't you do it, Ter? I can see it on the headstone: *She took her life as lovers often do*. Don McLean,' he added informatively.

'Anyway,' she said, 'I don't give a shit.'

'Any chance of a shot at that bottle, Ter?'

Reluctantly she passed it on, and it went around and came back almost empty. She swore loudly and shut up. When the joint came round next time she took it. I turned around to watch her, and as I watched I realised this was her first time. An excess of affection took me, and I wrapped my arms around her and hugged. She seemed to diminish in size as she pulled on the joint and the red tip intensified. She spluttered and coughed as she inhaled, so everybody laughed loudly. Afterwards she sheltered against me.

Later I heard the red Mini outside, and Kevin and Nuala came in. They were arguing, and their voices could be heard even before they got out of the car. I got up to see them, and it was only then that I realised the party was over. The kitchen was empty. A single couple was still dancing in the living room and the box player and the guitarist were finishing off what was left in the wine bottles. I told Kevin and Nuala they had missed a great party and left them to evict the remnants. The poet was asleep on my bed, so I woke him up and threw him out. Then Terry got up to go.

'So,' she said. 'So thanks anyway for the party.'

'Please don't go,' I said. 'Were you really going to kill yourself?'

She smiled. 'I'll stay as long as I can sleep in my clothes.'

I agreed and she got inside the blankets quickly. I stripped to the Jockeys and we curled against each other in the cold sheets. Our hands warmed each other, and slowly she allowed me to touch her. She had small soft breasts and when the nipples hardened they sprang away from the touch. Some time later we made love and fell into a deep and untroubled sleep. When I woke in the morning, she was gone but had left a note.

It's Sunday, in case you didn't know. Gone to mass.
Back for breakfast. Don't get up. Terry.

Charlie Kennedy arrived on the pretext of giving me back my essay. It was a wet Tuesday evening, and we had just managed to coax a fire into life in the living-room grate. It was the first time we had ever lit a fire there. That was Terry's doing. At the moment he called, she was kneeling in front of it, face and hands blackened and smelling of smoke.

'I brought back your essay.'

'Come on in. You know Terry.'

'Oh, I know Terry,' he said. Managing to make it as suspicious as possible. 'How've you been keeping, Terry?'

Terry told him to fuck off and carried on with the fire. Now she was holding the front page of *The Irish Times* against it and the draught was roaring in the chimney.

'Listen, I really came over to ask if you knew anything about Kevin.'

'Why?'

'Well, for starters, I haven't got an essay from him for weeks.' (I knew Kevin almost never turned in an essay. He had long ago decided he could do without the 10 per cent they represented on the paper.) 'But apart from that, I hear he's gone off the rails a bit. Knocking around with the Nuala. You know the way it is, they're bad for each other. That's what I'd say.'

In truth, I had seen little enough of Kevin. He slept here most nights, sometimes Nuala did too, but since Terry's arrival I had kept up a regular attendance at my courses, and so I was often out before he got up. The same was true for Terry. We often attended each other's lectures in fact. I wasn't sure what his condition was, but Charlie Kennedy's interest was strange.

'I'll tell him you were asking about him. He'll be surprised.'

'Overwhelmed,' Terry said. A brown circle was forming on *The Irish Times*.

I said, 'Watch out, Terry,' and almost immediately the paper caught fire. She dropped it straight into the grate and bundled it in with the fire tongs.

Charlie Kennedy looked like he was planning to stay, so I said I had work to do, thanked him for dropping back the essay and got him out.

'He makes me squirm,' Terry said. 'There's something behind all this. That bastard hasn't an ounce of humanity in his body. He reminds me of my ex-boyfriend.'

'The one who drove you to suicide?' I joked.

'That bastard. And it's no laughing matter.'

I cooked and Terry talked. If I remember rightly, it was a chilli or a curry. It was mostly beef we ate. By then you could buy steak for almost nothing down in the market because of the foot-and-mouth outbreak in England. I can remember the onions watering my eyes because Terry made a thing of wiping them with the sleeve of her blouse. I could smell her scent even over the smell of the onions.

She told me about her father, a schoolteacher in a small country school. She said everyone hated him, and hated her as a result. He would creep up behind them as they were writing and lift them out of their seats by the short hairs of their necks. That was his favourite trick, she said. And she always had to be best in her class. He started to beat her the day she went into first class, and to the day she left home he would take her pants down and flail her with his belt. If she struggled, as she rarely did, he would drive her around the room, sometimes even with a stick, or a brush handle, once even with a knife. If she escaped, he would take it out on her mother, so that in the end it was easier to take what he gave.

She learned never to shout or cry, because none of her friends knew. Nor could she tell them. The humiliation for a seventeen-year-old of being beaten like a child was too great to bear. She was sure that once the initial sympathy had worn off, she would merit only their contempt. And out of this certainty grew another certainty – that somehow she deserved it, if only because she never tried to escape.

The older locals respected him as much as the younger ones feared him. They called him the Master to his face or in his absence. It was an axiom in the parish that Master Kane put manners on the young pups. Not only did he put manners on them, but he found them work as well – farm labouring mostly for the boys, if they didn't have a farm of their own, shop assistant or checkout jobs in supermarkets for the girls. People could point to his creations as upstanding members of society.

But that wouldn't do for his own child.

'In the beginning he worked me till I hated him, but in the end I worked myself to get away. Than I hit this place and I just blew up. I suppose I'm completely fucked up now. I'm going to fail my finals and he'll kill me.'

Terry often said this, and now, as always, I comforted her as best I could, but I sensed something else in the way she said it, something that was beyond comforting, beyond restitution. It was as if failure were a kind of faith, as if she were simply repeating her belief like a prayer. And sometimes it seemed like a perverse hope.

Nevertheless, she went to lectures and wrote essays regularly. During all that time, she never missed one, never tried that trick with the bottle of Paddy again. And I take pride in that. We kept each other on the level in many ways. We stayed at home a lot and drank cheap wine from Galvin's off-licence, glutted on cheap beef and made love in front of the fire or went to bed early. We were tender to each other, both hurt, both healing in our own way. We were lonely and needed each other. I suppose we were simple, or naïve, having no thought for time and what it might bring.

She loved to drink while we made love, red wine like blood on her lips. And in her passion she used to say everything and cry like a child. Often as we approached the height, she would beg me never to hurt her, and her trust overwhelmed me.

Once I asked her why she continued to go to mass when she was living in sin. 'Insurance,' she said. 'Fire insurance.' We both laughed, but I knew it was too flippant to be true. She got up every Sunday morning. Sometimes she crept out so as not to wake me; sometimes even she was back before I noticed she'd gone. One evening she went to confession, and afterwards she talked about going back to her own place – a bedsit in the suburbs.

'But I need you,' I told her. 'I won't be able to do without you. I'll fail.' The last one was a cheap trick, using her own weakness against her.

'You don't need me as much as I need you,' she replied, 'and anyway if anyone is going to fail, it'll be me.'

I said she was behaving irrationally, that if there was a god he couldn't have any objection to us. I wanted to say that no matter what God wanted, I wanted her to stay. I wanted to say that God must be a cruel bastard if he would send each of us back to our separate loneliness after all. But mainly I wanted to hold her for ever, not to let her slip out of my fingers, out of my life.

And she didn't go.

Instead she began to feel guilty about our lovemaking. She would be reluctant for a time, capitulating reluctantly, afterwards sleeping uneasily. Things were not made easier by the fact that Kevin and Nuala were quarrelling a lot now. We still rarely saw them, but at night we could hear them from the next room. I knew they were both drinking more than they had been. They would stay out till the small hours, then ramble home, waking us as they came in, the house filled with the crazy pattern of their voices.

We tried not to know about it, but Terry fretted. And I began to feel that the house was somehow polluted, tainted, and that our love was being corrupted by the presence of Nuala and Kevin.

One day, after they had had a particularly bad row, Terry decided we had to get them out.

'They're freeloading on you. They're using this place as a

doss-house. You have to put them out. Jesus, they'll destroy you anyway. Take a look at yourself! You look like you haven't slept in a month. Which, as a matter of fact, you haven't.'

'I can't do it, Terry,' I told her. 'Kevin is my best friend. I can't do it.'

'Well, what about what he's doing to himself? She's a bitch if ever I saw one. Everybody knows about her and Charlie Kennedy. She'll eat him up.'

'What about her and Charlie Kennedy?'

Terry looked at me as if she had only now realised what a fool I was.

'Everyone knows she's with him when she's not here.'

'Jesus,' I said. 'I never knew you listened to the sca.'

It was meant to be cutting.

As it happened, I ran into them both at a political meeting shortly afterwards. It was Ógra Fianna Fáil, and we had gone along to heckle. There was a big crowd and there was a lot of enthusiasm and rhetoric. A student called MacCarthy was speaking when I arrived. He was talking about the great intellectual and moral loss that had befallen the party. That was because Dev had died that autumn after a decade or so of blindness and deafness as President of the Republic. MacCarthy kept referring to him as 'the Long Fellow', as if he knew him casually. There seemed to be a great deal of agreement, judging by the head-nodding and clapping, about how Dev had moulded a party of integrity and decency with the common man at its heart.

I heard shouting from the far end of the hall, well away from the exit, and almost immediately Kevin and Nuala burst from the crowd and rushed the podium. In a matter of seconds, the speaker was pushed aside and Kevin was shouting about Pol Pot. When the party lads began to jostle him offstage, he suddenly shouted that Dev was a wanker and a woman-hater. Somebody lashed out at him, and blood blossomed at the side of his nose. Nuala shouted and somebody else hit her. They were dragged down into the crowd, and gradually the mayhem reached the door. When they were ejected, I followed and found Nuala gasping for breath and Kevin sitting on a step. Inside, the uproar was dying down and MacCarthy was voicing the spirit of the nation, and lo and behold who also spilled out but Charlie Kennedy. He spoke quietly to Nuala while I held a handkerchief to Kevin's nose. They laughed over something. When Kevin was ready to get up, Charlie Kennedy was gone. Kevin said, 'Where's that fuckin' shifty bastard Charlie Kennedy?'

Nuala shrugged.

Apart from a bloody nose and a few bruises, Kevin was OK, and Nuala was only winded. I took them up to Ludgate's for a pint. Bill Ludgate wasn't too happy about serving me – we had had some differences a year previously – but I told him it was medicinal and that we'd be out as soon as health had been restored, so he left us alone. We went into the small room where there was a blazing fire.

They talked all that night about the trip to Kerry. They hadn't forgotten it. It was still on. That is, if Terry and I would come. They wouldn't go on their own. The only problem was money. They had gone through Kevin's grant, more or less, and Nuala was getting fewer and fewer hours in the takeaway. A lot of it went on drink, but they had bought books as well, and clothes. Kevin had a fantastic pair of boots, and Nuala had silver earrings. If they could get enough money together, they'd take off tomorrow, enough for petrol for the Mini, and a few nights B & B. They'd hit Kerry like a hurricane.

Terry Kane, according to Nuala, was the most wonderful woman in the country. I was incredibly lucky. She mentioned

John Lennon and Thomas Hardy by way of comparison. I had noticed before that Nuala's field of reference was very broad. Now she told me she hoped Terry was a good fuck because I deserved it. *She* was, she said emphatically, which was more than Kevin deserved, and any time I could change places and she'd have the better bargain. By then we were all very drunk. We made our way back to the flat with a couple of six-packs and woke Terry up.

Kevin had some dope, and we drank and smoked until we all felt elated and exhausted at once. I seem to remember Nuala and Terry singing something in duet. Kevin gave a fireworks display by turning out the lights and twirling a lighted cigarette very fast so as to make magic shapes in front of our slow-motion eyes, and I recited the first part of 'Kubla Khan', a poem which had never failed to get a response in such circumstances because everyone knew it was supposed to be about an opium dream. Terry and I went to bed very late and woke in the same mood of elation. We stayed in bed all morning and went out about two o'clock to get something to eat in the Kampus Kitchen. There Nuala tracked us down, demanding that we pack our bags. We were going to Kerry.

None of us had enough money to stay in the guesthouse, booked by Nuala as the cheapest dive in Kerry. Fortunately we had brought sleeping bags as a precaution against what she called Kerry Damp, a kind of rising bog which she claimed infected every bed in Kerry. We spent the nights sleeping in turns, twisted impossibly into the backseat of the Mini. We woke up in a different place each morning, but always facing out to the taunting clarity of the Atlantic air. Our clothes got damp as the dew slipped in through the leaky bodywork, and our bones got cold and stiff. On the third morning, the Mini refused to start, but fortunately we had parked at the top of a headland, so we pushed it until it spat smoke and jerked away from us. Naturally we all fought like sharks, and like sharks the suggestion of a hurt to one of us drove the others into a frenzy of cruelty. We made it worse by drinking in the pubs until the very last moment, unconsciously or consciously postponing the minute when we would have to look at the Mini and say, 'Well, whose turn is it?'

The days were different though, as if a malevolent spirit settled on us at lighting-up time; the days were crystal clear, brilliant with light shattered off the sea. We bought cooked chickens and beer and ate them on the sand, tearing the chickens apart with our hands. Afterwards we played football with a can or walked along the foreshore. There was the privacy of the marram and the warm joints of sand between the rocks. And there was always so much to make up, so much to say, and it all gave the days depth and turned them into idylls.

Once we talked about our childhoods. We had all been Catholics; Terry in a way still was. Nuala came of party stock – Fine Gael, farming and the confraternity, as she said. Kevin and myself were both solid middle-class, middle Ireland. We marvelled at how badly our conditioning had gone astray.

'Here we are,' Kevin said, 'flaad out on a beach in Kerry, littering the place with chicken bones and empty bottles of Harp . . .'

'Not to mention the sex,' I added.

'The sex,' he said, 'is only fucking outrageous.' Or words to that effect. 'And not a whiff of that shithead Charlie Kennedy.'

I said nothing. He wagged his finger at me.

'I know your type. I know what you're doing, you shagging literary wanker! Thinking about God. Or better again, not thinking about God.'

'If the fellows at the office could see me now.'

Nuala sat up suddenly. She had been stretched out with her hands over her eyes, the winter sun glaring down on her.

'What difference is there?' she said. There was an edge in her voice.

'There's a world of a difference,' I said. 'Jesus.'

'So you smoke dope,' she said. 'You make love in the grass when there's no one looking. So you read Sartre and all that other shit. But deep down you're the same. So is Kevin. So am I.'

'None of us are the same,' I cried. I was hurt by it. And added, lamely, 'None of us are the same as our parents.'

'Prove it,' she said.

'How? If it isn't obvious anyway.'

'It isn't obvious.' There was a smile shimmering at the edge of her lips now. 'I'll show you how.'

She stood up and looked at the sea. Then slowly she took off her clothes and kicked them into a bundle. We lay there staring at her until she stood totally naked so that we could see the winter raising gooses on her sides. Then she began to walk slowly down to the water, without stopping, without looking back. I remember with absolute clarity the sound of the waves tumbling on to the sand and broken shells at the water's edge, the colour of her hair against the light, the way her ass dimpled at the thighs when her leg swung back. We were enthralled.

She stepped in gingerly, testing, then she turned and it seemed she was coming back, but she turned again and went in and didn't stop this time until she plunged in head first.

We were excited by her courage and ashamed not to be following her. Her beauty paralysed us. We stared frankly, but nobody spoke until she was dressed again. Then she said that if we hadn't the courage to do that, we couldn't say we had left it all behind. Soon she began to shiver, and being nearest I gave her my sweater. As I laid it on her back, I felt my arms were enclosing an incredible animal, as pure and as fearless as a unicorn.

'You know,' she said, 'Terry is the only one of us who is different. Look at her. She's totally naked.'

I looked at Terry then and saw that she had been crying. Her face was streaked still, even as she brushed at it. She and Nuala embraced, their arms locked tightly into the flesh, and Kevin and I, sensing that they were beyond us in some way, got up and kicked a can around on the sand between the rocks and the sea.

That night was warmer than the others, the kind of pet night not unusual in the south. Clouds had come in and there was a suggestion of rain in the air. Terry and I walked along the headland and sat staring out at the blackness of the horizon, listening to the waves roll along and expend themselves on the rocks. Occasional phosphorescence winked at us.

'She's beautiful, isn't she?' Terry said.

I was cautious. 'This is a change,' I said. 'Where's the Whore of Babylon we were talking about a few days ago?'

Terry looked fixedly out across the rocks. After a while, as if I hadn't interrupted, she said, 'And she has no shame or no inhibitions. She's lucky. I wish I was her.'

'You're wrong there,' I said. 'Not to want to have shame. It's eating her up.'

She thought I was dramatising.

'Just because she drinks too much all the time.'

'And smokes too much and fucks too much. And all that. But that's not why I'm saying it. I mean it. She's dying.'

'Of shamelessness?' Terry roared with laughter. She laughed so much she fell back against the heather the better to laugh at the sky. I waited until she was finished and had wiped the water from her eyes.

'Zo,' I joked in a German accent, 'ze cause of death? Ze Shvine hat no shem.'

'I suppose,' Terry said, serious this time. 'I suppose she's a kind of whore all right. But everybody wants a whore, isn't that true? Isn't that what Freud said? Everybody has to have two women: one is a virgin and the other is a whore. One is innocent and trusting and dependent, and the other is dangerous and desirable. One is for sex and the other is for home.'

I said, 'Freud thought that was a disease.'

'So what? Some people need their diseases.'

'Nobody is really like what Freud thought they were.'

'Some people are,' she said. 'Oh yes they are.'

We heard their cries from across the strand on the way back, and Terry looked intently at me. For the first time I found her gaze unbearable. But they were fighting and the car looked as if it were going to collapse, or else the handbrake would slip and the car would drift down into the water. If it had done so, they would certainly not have noticed.

It was probably that night, as we strove to sleep in the cramp of the car, four of us sprawled against each other between the fretwork of the steering wheel and the immense mound of the door handle, legs on the handbrake, arms over heads, the gear lever always in the wrong place; it was probably that night that Nuala told us about her sister.

'Margaret is her name. And she's four years older than me. Wild, too. All the girls in our family were wild, even though I'm the worst. She used to sneak out to go dancing at Redbarn, when my parents thought she was still in bed. She had a special miniskirt for the occasion, short almost as far as her ass. She kept it laid out under her mattress, so it was always ready when needed, as she said. She used to walk the mile to the main road in a pair of Wellington boots, with this miniature mini under her ordinary skirt, and when she got to the crossroads, she used to hide them in a hole in the ditch until she came home again. Then she'd put on her high heels and stash the outside skirt. A minibus used to drive round the villages and the crossroads to pick people up for the dance. There were showbands. Dickie Rock and Joe Mac. Everybody loved Joe Mac because he used to tell dirty jokes and do rip-offs of people. And the guy who drove the minibus was an ageing Teddy boy – slicked hair and pointy toes and all. He used to make passes at the women in the bus – it was always women. I don't know how the fellas got there, but it wasn't in that bus. They had cars I suppose, or bicycles. Margaret used to say that the smell of a woman's underarm was all he wanted. When he'd get them to the Barn, he used to ask the girls to let him smell them, and if they let him, he'd go off happy into the trees.

'Anyway, the Barn was this huge dance hall on the edge of a huge sandy beach, and all the couples used to go down into the sand. That's why my father never let Margaret go to the dances. So she used to sneak out. Well, as I said, Margaret was the wild one. She used to tell me every morning who she went dancing with last night. And if I was really lucky, she'd even tell me what he did. All I remember was a lot of hot French kissing. Sometimes, if he was the rushing type, he'd shove his knee in between her legs and that'd probably satisfy him. He'd go back to his farm in the hills and cream off for a month thinking about it. It was all push and shove, roving hands and slaps, and tickles and bites. I used to think – I was thirteen or so at the time – that if sex was like that, I'd rather play camogie.

'I used to hear the minibus coming back, and if it was a calm night with a light breeze from the south, I could hear fragments of their voices across the fields. I used to stay awake on purpose to hear them. The countryside is lonely at night for a young girl. Nothing to break it up except the sound of a dog barking or a fox, or a distant car.

'One night she came straight into my room to tell me about it. She'd finally met someone she actually liked. He was an accountant in a firm in Youghal. After that she slipped out all the more often. I was amazed that she got away with it. She'd tell my mother she was going upstairs to study – that was the year of her Leaving Cert – and then she was going straight to bed. Then she'd get out through the window and meet him some-place in his car. Several times I thought about telling; in fact I threatened it more than once, but always something happened to put her back in favour. She might say that Dominic, the accountant, had sent me a box of chocolates – it was always Irish Rose – or she'd let me in on some detail of what they were doing. I remember when I first found out it was gone beyond the French kissing. It was a casual remark of hers, that he hated bra fasteners or something, or that he had cold hands, but it set me thinking and dreaming. For the first time I began to consid-er what a man's hands would be like. I went through all the usual discoveries then, in the space of a few weeks. Or at least it seems like that now. And during that time, I developed an obses-sion about spying on them. I followed her one night – I couldn't stand it any longer. It was springtime, and it wasn't so dark as it had been, so it was easy enough. I saw them in the car together, and I saw the fake struggle she put up. I saw him lift her sweater, and I saw him go down on her breasts. She threw her head back and her mouth opened slightly, and even from where I was hid-ing, I could hear her breathing. I lost my courage and ran home as fast as my legs could carry me.

'Of course, guess what happened? Thanks be to Christ for the pill! She got pregnant, and he married her with very little persuasion. They make a nice pair. Good to each other and everything. Three children. She was the youngest lady captain of the golf club a couple of years ago.'

Nuala said nothing for a while. Then she slapped her fist off the dashboard. 'I hate that fucking bitch,' she shouted. 'And her prick of a husband! She had the neck to tell me I should get a grip on myself! Jesus fucking Christ! She said I was throwing myself away.'

We went to Considine's Pub & Ballad Lounge most nights we were in Kerry because there was good music, and they had a square of timber in the middle of the floor where you could get up and dance. Nuala and Terry knew all the dances, mostly polkas and slides, and they spent an hour or two dragging us on and off the floor and showing us the steps. Kevin came off badly, but I began to get the hang of it, at least to the extent that my feet were in the right place at more or less the right time.

One night we found ourselves in an argument with three men at the next table. We were talking about Seán Ó Riada. We were saying that he had put life back in Irish music. That people like The Dubliners and Planxty would never have got off the ground without him.

I had had a drop too much and felt sentimental and inspired. I said his love of music killed him. That Ireland was a sow eating her litter. I think I may even have quoted Kinsella's elegy: *I am in great danger, he said* . . . I had heard Kinsella himself read it not long before. Certainly I was lyrical about it.

The talk turned to the Provos, as all talk of culture in Ireland must eventually turn. It transpired that the men we were talking to *were* Provos. One had been over the border. The older one had been out in the fifties campaign. He reminisced about jumping ditches with a bag of revolvers to avoid the Special Branch car that was coming for him.

Naturally we kicked ourselves under the table and put our heads down into our pints and paid attention to the music. True or not, trouble would be big trouble if it came. There was no sense in drawing the local *boys* down on us.

But Nuala suddenly produced a block of hash that nobody knew she had and began to offer it around.

'Look,' she said to the one who had been out in the fifties, 'you can put it in your pipe! I never tried it that way, but I'd say it's brilliant! Even if it isn't a water pipe. That's what you need,' she nudged him and winked, 'a hookah! You wouldn't be so uptight about Mother Ireland if you smoked shit.'

She was brittle and dangerous like that, as dangerous for us, at least, as the men were. But the Fifties Man scowled at us and turned his back. One of the others called us fucking hippies, and said did we know that it was people like us that were sapping the courage of the people? Drug addicts and degenerates. Over the border, he told us, they'd kneecap us. Nuala told him she knew a Kerryman who thought that *kneecap him* was the Irish for *I don't think,* and tried to explain the joke when they didn't laugh.

For the rest of the night we managed to keep her under control. She danced a lot, increasingly wildly, drawing attention to herself more than we wanted, but she kept away from the Provos. They drank their pints and stared at her from time to time. I met one of them in the toilet and he looked out of it. He was leaning his head against the wall of the urinal to steady himself. I remember he pissed down the leg of his trousers. I began to relax. As drunk as that, there was no danger in them. I started to enjoy myself again. I took Nuala out for a waltz and she pressed against me as if I were her lover, and I couldn't keep my hands still. She looked up at me once, and I said, 'I can't help it, Nuala. You're so beautiful.'

And she just smiled and told me to carry on, and said if she didn't like it she'd have stopped me long ago.

'But take your time,' she told me. 'I like it slow. Remember that.'

At closing time we took the remains of our pints out into the open and finished them off in the shocking cold of the street. It seemed to us that the air and the stars cleared our heads, and we talked and talked out there until the cold got inside our clothes. We stood our empty glasses on the windowsills and wrapped our arms tightly round our chests and sucked the night in.

The Mini was parked along by the quays, and the three Provos were standing beside it.

'Jesus Christ, Kevin, they're waiting for us.'

'We can't run now,' he said. 'They'd catch us. They'd wreck the car. *And* we'd have to come back sooner of later.'

'Good night, lads and lassies,' the Fifties Man said.

Someone, probably the drunk one, had puked on the front windscreen. The third was sitting on the bonnet and bouncing up and down.

'Why couldn't you buy an Irish car as you were at it?' the Fifties Man laughed. 'A Ford. Made in Cork, where you come from yourselves. This old yoke'll never stand up to the climate around here.'

Nuala saw the puke and exploded.

'Get off my fucking car, you bastards! I'll fucking kill you.'

She rushed them before we could stop her, and the Fifties Man had her in his arms in an instant.

'Fucking hippie.' He was very strong. 'Listen boys,' he told us, 'why don't you shag off and leave the ladies here? Or even if you want to take the other one, we'll keep this one. Sure we could see straight away the kind she was.'

'Yah,' said the drunk, 'she's a whore all right.'

'A fine half,' the third added conversationally.

Kevin went for the Fifties Man with fists flailing, and then the drunk stepped in. He was lighter than I imagined he would be, fast as a cat. His blow struck Kevin on the cheek and seemed to lift him backwards slightly. A second blow caught him on the ear and he fell down. He retreated quickly from a badly aimed kick and the drunk laughed.

'I destroyed the car,' he said, 'but you know the way it is. Sure a feed of drink can't be always good. I always said Considine's stuff was sour. But I'm a lot better now. I got it off me chest.'

'I'm getting a feeling about you, me lassie,' said The Fifties Man. 'Down here.'

He shoved one hand between her legs and she started to scream. He tried to shut her up but she bit him. I could see the others were panicking.

'Jaze,' said the third man, 'shut her up or she'll have the guards out.'

Terry began to scream then as well, and Kevin and I shouted for all we were worth. Lights began to go on in the cottages along the quay.

The Fifties Man shoved Nuala back, and the others began to run.

'We know where you are,' he told us.

He punched Nuala on the breast and shoved her against the car. Then they were gone. We could hear the thump of their feet echoing from a side street. They were gone so quickly I almost didn't notice.

Nuala cried all the way back to Tráigh an Fhíona. Kevin drove and Terry hugged her in the back seat. She had to change her clothes because of the smell, and since she had washed some things in the sea that morning and they weren't yet dry, she had to put on some of everybody's. Then we all sat out, wrapped in our sleeping bags, and talked. Nuala broke up some cigarettes and rolled a third of the dope into a joint. We smoked another after that and it calmed us. We lay back and looked up at the stars, and ribbed Nuala about not telling us she had it before. Then we pooled all the sleeping bags and got in under them and fell asleep locked in each others' arms. The dew woke us, and our clothes and sleeping bags were wet through. It was six o'clock, and dawn was still a long way off. We got into the Mini and drove home, as much for the warmth of the heater as to escape.

Terry

My father is here. I heard a knock at the door. Jim is out, but it isn't his knock. I know it's Daddy. He has a firm knock, practised. A hand that knocked on doors to complain about truancy, or to say he had found a place for someone. The Master's hand. The first thought that comes into my mind is *Will he beat me?* I don't know what I would do if he beat me here. Once, when I was about fourteen, he heard I was smoking. The nuns told him. We used to smoke in the toilets, and we always had a first-year to keep watch. But the first-year ran away instead of warning us and we were caught. For the others it was an embarrassment, the fear of being kept in at night, extra homework. But my father was waiting for me when I came home. He had a letter in his hand, and I could see the convent motto, probably hand-delivered by the same first-year that ran away. He caught me by the ears and pulled me into the kitchen. My mother was sitting at the table as pale as a sheet, folding and unfolding her hands. He stood me up against the sink, and he seemed quite calm. I didn't look at his face, but he seemed to be different, without rage, almost sad. I wondered if I was going to escape this time. Then, without warning and in total silence, he began to strike me – in the stomach, on the chest, on the shoulders – careful as he could be not to leave marks, though he didn't always succeed. Then in a pause he was telling me, quite calmly, that he was suffering for my sin of disobedience, that what I had done was a shame to my family, that he regretted having to hurt me, that to spare the rod was to spoil the child. When I was crumpled up against the sink, he kicked me and tried to stand me up again. I didn't cry loudly because my best friend was waiting for me out on the street. She might knock on the door at any moment, and someone would have to explain to her, or he might even make me go out and tell her to go away, and she would see quite plainly what was happening to me.

Nothing ever came out of those beatings. I never became resolved about leaving home. I never grew suddenly courageous like someone in a film or those powerful women who phone radio talk shows. In a way I became more cowardly, more shamed, more hypocritical. When the whole school discovered that someone's father had gone to England and was living with some woman, I threw in my lot with the jeerers. I took as much pleasure as I could out of making veiled remarks to her and sniggering afterwards because she didn't seem to notice. I laughed when a friend got pregnant, and I pretended to be helping her so as to get the inside information for the other smokers in the school toilets.

And my father never became contrite and tearful like the psychology books say. He never apologised to my mother or me, or anyone else that he harmed. Instead he got a heart attack one day as his class was doing a geography exercise, and had to retire at the early age of sixty-three. Retirement didn't suit him, and he spent his time stalking up and down the village and writing bitter letters to the newspapers in Irish.

I almost never see him. When I have to go home, I do – Christmas holidays or for a family funeral. Not much else to draw me back. There is always the excuse of my studies, which he seems to accept. He has never enquired about my results. When I say my holidays end at such and such a day, he doesn't raise his head from the newspaper. My mother looks away and doesn't speak.

Now he is sitting at my table, drinking tea from Jim's mug, looking caved in a little, slightly hollow-faced. He wants to know who I am sharing my flat with. He looks around in the pause that follows his question and precedes my answer, a pause too long I know, but I have not prepared an answer, never even expected to have to give one, don't know whether I will tell him or tell him a lie such as I have grown used to telling.

His eye rests on Jim's dark green jacket, and I see him calculating that such a jacket could never fit me, even with my taste for outsizes. (And as I see all this, I see Jim's hunched back in the jacket and the way he turned his face towards me, myopic and bland, as if the book he was studying had robbed him of reality.) Then he notices that the mug has *Jim's Mug* glazed in green along the side opposite the handle. A present from Dingle. He puts it down quietly and looks at me. Waiting for an answer.

Why should I answer him?

Why should I tell him one word.

Fuck him.

I could tell him Jim will never be back.

I could say I think Nuala has him. That I've seen them dancing together and that her body is incredibly beautiful and that I don't blame Jim for wanting her instead of me.

I say, 'His name is Jim.' I point at the mug. 'Obviously.'

He straightens up. The quiet look is there again. He reaches down into the pocket of his overcoat (does he have a cane?) and his hand slowly fishes up a handkerchief. He blows his nose.

'You're going to come with me, miss. I took the precaution of finding a flat for you, not quite so near the college. I would bring you home to your mother this minute except that I have invested so much in your education and you might as well finish it. The landlady is an elderly widow, a Mrs O'Donoghue, the sister of a man from home. I was instrumental in procuring a place for her daughter in the Civil Service, so I can trust her completely. A good Christian woman. I hope you haven't lost your head completely? You're not, aha, expecting? Mrs O'Donoghue drew the line at that. She has no wish to draw shame on herself.'

He blows his nose again. In the time he is speaking, he keeps the handkerchief poised in front of his face, casual, cold. But I see now that there's a tremor in his hands. *Parkinson's Disease*, I think. Somebody told me all old people get it. In this case, too late. Certainly not fear.

'Don't pack anything. In case your – paramour' (he coughs and laughs a small tight laugh) 'should barge in on us. The man who owns the mug. I'll come back myself for everything.'

He drives me about two miles as far as a place called Summerton Avenue or Summerton Close. Unbelievably the house is called Xanadu. A small fat woman opens the door. She has bad teeth, and as I shake hands with her I smell rather than hear her words. My room has a single bed with not enough blankets, a kettle on a tin tray and a cup and saucer. A large wardrobe with a mirror on the door, a straight-backed chair. I am to eat my meals with Mrs O'Donoghue, the keeper of the keys. I may not leave the house or enter it without her permission. The door closes at nine-thirty, ten on Saturdays. No Drink. No Men. No

Pets. No Food in the Rooms. My father will drive up each week to make sure I'm still here. Mrs O'Donoghue will telephone if there is a breach of discipline. She knows everything. No secrets.

As soon as they go, I climb into the wardrobe and close the door. There is a comfort in the smell of darkness and camphor balls. In the fact that outside the darkness is a mirrored door. After a time I get out and pull the blankets off the bed. I take them into the wardrobe with me. I roll them into a ball behind my back and go to sleep.

What I'm really worried about is what happens when she's finished with Charlie Kennedy. And Kevin. I mean, I can hold out indefinitely. But I saw her dancing with Jim. He couldn't keep his hands to himself. And she liked it. I could see that, too. She's animal in a way. She just needs to be stroked in the right places. Like my dog. If you scratched him under the hard part of his ear, he would go quiet and his eyes would go glazed, almost hooded. I've seen her like that too.

Jim would like to fuck her. He won't do it as long as I'm around. But he becomes attached easily. Look at the way he took to me. He kind of grows on people, like ivy. After a time, to break him loose you have to rip things out. If she goes for him he'll take her, I know it.

Then what will I do?

Mrs O'Donoghue doesn't know I managed to smuggle some shit in here last night. I waited till she went to bed and I smoked it all. I bombed out totally, and I thought I could see Jim and Nuala in bed.

She has one of those model bodies, like they hang clothes on in shop windows. Her breasts are bigger than mine. I think I have arrested development. The strange thing is that while I was watching them I was enjoying myself. I wasn't jealous at all.

Does this mean I would like to go to bed with her, too?

I have sex on the brain.

Because I'm not getting any.

What about Mrs O'D?

Mrs O'D says the sheets on my bed are the ones she laid her late husband out on. 'Wilful waste,' she says, 'makes woeful want.'

Saw Jim.

'What happened, Terry?'

I was a bit out of it. Mrs O'D doesn't recognise the aroma of cannabis resin. I've cut a square hole out of *A Critique of Pure Reason*. I get the hit by snapping the book open, inhaling quickly and snapping it closed again. Almost nothing escapes. Who showed me how to do that?

'Terry.'

I can remember telling him to fuck off, himself and Nuala. I can remember him going, too. In the light of a little reason, I can see I was wrong. But who cares!

Whatever it was, it's over.

Everything is over. Most things anyway. I'll do it this time. One of these days.

I have been permitted a visitor. Because she was female. Needless to say it was Nuala, and she brought, of all things, a poem from Jim. Mrs O'D told her I was studying too hard altogether. That she wasn't happy about the bags under my eyes. 'Her father is very hard on her,' she said. 'The Master is a hard man.' She told Nuala she could stay the night because Nuala said she had driven up from home. She even put cushions and blankets on the floor.

The poem was about love and pain and things that can't

endure and was heavily influenced by Leonard Cohen. It started with a quotation from Dante in Italian.

'Let's get locked,' Nuala said. I tapped my nose. Mrs O'D would guess. Instead we smoked from the square hole in Kant's *Critique*. Nuala made love to me, of course. I expected that. When she began to take my clothes off, I felt suddenly powerful, as if I had willed it. I felt as if every muscle, every nerve ending, was so electric that anything they brushed against would implode. So I touched her perfect body as tenderly as I could, not wanting to destroy her.

The act itself disappointed me. It was pointless, singular, unforgiving, but afterwards my head was comfortable and at home against the crook of her neck. It would have been the perfect end if Mrs O'D had come in with a nice tray of tea and toast to find us naked together, a siren and a child, asleep in her funeral sheets.

The Bestiary

It strikes him then that there are portents, that anything may be a sign – objects and their arrangements, their disposition in regard to other things, the colour, the texture – that the world is a wilderness of significance. For an instant he is uncertain of his place in the lecture, the words on the paper dissolving, their edges bleeding into each other. He hears the pens scrabbling, the shuffling of feet, the whispering. His head is saturated with sounds, and there is no place for the word. He sets his finger down and follows the finger to the paper and finds that the letters are disjointed, blurring, more like watery hieroglyphs or random etchings on a rough plate.

Which is it? he wonders. *Hieroglyphs or random marks? Is there a message?*

He is assailed by the knowledge of his own inadequacy, his unpreparedness, his lack of skill in the kind of ciphering required to understand these phenomena. He listens carefully and hears a tiny scrabbling sound, and behind that, a distant susurration akin to water on a pebbly shore or voices whispering in a nearby room. Panic grips him again, but only for a moment. This time a name reaches out to him from the page. *Tradescant.* It has a comforting bourgeois sound, an ordinariness that reassures him. John Tradescant extends his hand through four hundred years to rescue him from confusion. Something concrete. Like his own name: Tom Ryan, meet John Tradescant.

He has a fleeting picture of the elder Tradescant, the royal gardener, tramping heavily through his park of curiosities *circa*

1650, plants brought from distant lands (so many suffixed *tradescantia*), the wonder of all England.

After all, he thinks, *I am a little overwrought, no more. I need a holiday. Perhaps I need glasses.* The thought comes to him that he may be lonely, hence the phenomenon of a middle-aged lecturer who seeks out the comforting presence of the long-dead, a bachelor in a third-class university plundering history for companionship. But on the other hand, what else would a scholar be?

He looks up now, fills the lacuna with a dissembling cough, and raises his voice to tell them that their research must reach as far as the Tradescants, *père et fils*, the first rumblings of the bizarre as a public obsession, not just the preserve of scientists and royal collectors. The phrasing pleases him. This is the controversial subject of one his first scholarly articles, snarled over by experts in the field at the time, his own pet theory.

He is in full flight then, silencing the scrabbling, the voices. The disturbing awareness of meaning in everything that has elated and depressed him in recent weeks fades away. He is never so happy as at a lecture, he tells himself, ignoring the cold sweat that is starting at his armpits. He pulls the comforting name out again. Tradescant. And the anxiety is stilled.

'They were not just botanists who gave their names to a number of useful garden plants, but also, I contend, the originators in English literature to the present day of our fascination with the bizarre. If I tell you that their public collection of curiosities included, and I quote –' He shuffles his papers dramatically, not needing to, but enjoying the tiny hiatus, sensing the poised pens and eager eyes '– *two feathers of the Phoenix tayle and a natural dragon above two inches long.* That's from the catalogue of 1656. You get the significance?'

When it came out, his article had caused a satisfying controversy, but in the end the scholarly consensus was simple: he was wrong. They had no doubt about it and proceeded to ignore the thesis in all future work. At least that was how he saw it. Not for him the scholar's modest pleasure of seeing his name quoted in footnotes. It was a kind of oblivion. Nothing he had written since had raised so many hackles or, for that matter, come close to reaching the footnote threshold.

He stares up at the stacked theatre, the benches rising tier upon tier, nuns in the front, louts at the back, the great mass of those who could not do and would teach instead in between. From where he stands, their heads are on an elevated plane so that although they bend assiduously to their work he is looking directly into their faces. Mostly girls. One or two beauties as always. What brought them to a module on Beasts and Horrors as Motifs in English Literature (10 lectures)?

'I'm going to leave it there for today because, as you know, there is a reception in the Staff Common Room where an unconscionable quantity of free wine is available for those who appreciate such things.'

He stops again. He does not intend to go to the reception, but he likes them to think of him as a Rabelaisian reveller. In fact, he will hurry home to his study. He shivers at the thought: the tiny echoing room, the blank paper, the gloomy books, the noise. He wonders if perhaps he has rats hiding somewhere in the cavities or under the floorboards, their scrabbling echoing through his conscious thoughts even when he is away from home. He shakes his head briefly to banish them and sees one or two students nodding to each other.

They watch every move I make, he thinks. *I have begun to develop tics. I must stop shaking my head.*

'As regards free drink, students need not apply.'

There is a ripple of laughter. They like his wit.

'Let me just recommend something hot off the presses and

not available in the library. Marina Warner's new book, *It's No Go the Bogeyman*. I suggest sleeping with a rich medical student who'll buy it in hardback for you as a gift.'

The joke goes down well. Chuckles as the class breaks up, the louts making for the door, heavy-booted, talking loudly about football; nuns gathering paraphernalia; people moving up and down the theatre steps. The fleeting impression of a vast companionability.

He sees an angular girl in black leggings, black padded plastic jacket, hair cut tight. She swings down through the moving crowd, a counter-flow, and the crowd separates to let her through. She is looking directly at him.

'Excuse me,' she says while still two steps up from the floor. 'About this Tradescant guy.'

He smiles and nods. She takes the last two steps quickly and suddenly is standing in front of him, legs splayed, one hand in the pocket of her jacket, one clenched in a tight little fist at her side. He sees no evidence of an A4 pad.

'What I want to find out is, is this guy Tradescant worth chasing up? I mean does he exist even?'

'Oh yes,' he says. 'John Tradescant exists all right. Existed, I should say. In fact, there were two of him, father and son. In fact, his collection was the foundation of the Ashmolean Museum in Oxford.'

'Only I don't want to go after some fucking gardener, do I?'

He is taken aback by her language and answers severely, professorially: 'But we are not interested in the people here; we're after the roots of the metaphor.'

'Yeah, right,' she says. Standard modern expression of disbelief. 'Only I chased up Lyly that you mentioned last week. What a boring fucking book. *Euphues*. I mean we're talking about the Barbara Cartland of the fucking sixteenth century here.'

'But very influential,' he parries. The lecture theatre is empty and his voice has a curious hollow reverberation. 'I quote: *That beautie in Court which could not parley Euphuism, was as little regarded as she which now there speakes not French.* Charles Blount.'

'Yeah, right. Whoever he is.'

She is bored.

'Look, I have this reception I mentioned.'

'Yeah, right. The free wine.'

'Exactly. The free wine.'

'Only, this is the third lecture,' she says, 'and you're still in the fucking Dark Ages.'

He wants to say that it's not the fucking Dark Ages, and that the whole point of his course is to establish the roots of literary horror in its historical context and that she will have to wait another five lectures before he comes within an ass's roar of the twentieth century. But he is aware of his own blind spot. *I'm comfortable enough in the past*, he thinks. *It's the present that worries me.*

'Well, stick around,' he tells her. 'If you can take another two or three hundred years of gardeners. And let me remind you, apropos the references and so on, that the failure rate in my class is just over 30 per cent per annum.'

Her look is withering, an incipient snarl rucking the upper lip. She sighs and swings away from him. He watches her go up the steps. One of those aggressive students that he gets sometimes, crossovers from some other discipline, commerce or psychology, where they have an unshakeable conviction that a few units of Eng Lit will teach their students to write better reports. Horror always draws them. She won't last long. She was probably attracted to his course because she thought he would cover Stephen King. Her patience will wear out.

She turns at the top, one hand holding the swing-door. She calls down to him as he gathers up his papers and opens the mouth of his leather case.

'I'll check it out,' she says. 'I'm probably the only one in the place who follows up your fucking references.'

And she is gone.

He detects a faint shimmer where she has been, like a ripple in space, an after-image of the door and her body, their angular shapes thrown into some hieratic relationship.

Who is she?

The air is suddenly charged with sex: rank and saucy, potent, confounding him.

Three nights he dreams of her. When he wakes after the first night, there are some lines of poetry in his head: 'Sure thou wast born a whore even from the womb of some rank bawd, unsavoury as a tomb, who, carted from all parishes, did sell forbidden fruits in the highway to hell.'

Thomas Carew, he thinks. *What put that there?*

He remembers his dream. She is on her knees, her leggings dragged down around her thighs. He ruts into her, sweating, and as he ruts she talks, foulness streaming from her.

The smell.

But what is the end of the poem? He finds it in his study, a forgotten anthology: *Minor Poets of the Seventeenth Century.* 'And let no man ever bemoan thy case that once did know thee in the state of grace.'

He holds the book close to his face and scrutinises it. By now he knows how it works. There is always some way to reach him. It is up to him to be alert. The dream, the poem, the book are indices. He must bend all his thought to elucidate them. He holds the book to the light of the window. There are marks in the margin, almost-letters, half-characters. The smell, too, is important. Dry paper? A suggestion of glue?

An hour passes in study, the background filling with the sound of small things in the woodwork, distant insinuating voices. When he puts the book down to rub his palms over tired eyes, he takes the time to listen and can distinguish occasional words: strumpet, Ishmaelite, infanticide, grace. Isolated cells of innuendo. The connective tissue between them is lost, burned off in a fever of listening and reading. When he puts the book away, the noise is suffocating. He shakes his head, but there is no diminution. He rushes into his clothes, catches up his coat and bag and goes, slamming the door behind him.

The crash restores silence.

It is the quiet time, mid-hour, in the student restaurant. Tom queues patiently while a pair of girls argue with the person at the coffee urn about getting decaf. In the end the woman shrugs her shoulders and says, 'It's what they gives me, girl; I don't buy it meself.' The two girls glare at each other and ask for glasses of water. He notices that they have oozing burgers on their trays, a pile of flaccid chips, sachets of ketchup, paper packets of salt and a pool of urine-coloured vinegar.

He takes his tray (tea and a Danish pastry) to the furthest table, his briefcase jammed under one arm. He lowers the tray carefully and drops the briefcase. It falls with a dead sound, papers rather than books. There was a time when he always carried a book with him, when he was still alive with the discovery of each new joy, when he was still publishing regularly – poetry and scholarly articles. A time when he would take two or three days in Dublin – the Folklore Commission, the Chester Beatty, lunch with someone else in the field from Trinity or UCD. Today he takes his lecture notes out and arranges them on the table in front of him as a blind, hoping to appear busy. He clips the top off his pen and puts it beside them.

An alibi, he thinks. *I need an alibi for being here. The truth is these papers represent idleness, not work, intellectual rigor mortis. I have ceased to think. Someone said it about Ronald Reagan – that the lights were on but there was no one home.*

He cuts the Danish in four, the thought of Reagan reminding him that Henry Kissinger always had a half-dozen for breakfast, and is about to pick up the first piece when he sees her come in. She saunters uncertainly to the counter and buys a coffee. He specifically hears her ask for instant, significantly cheaper than the black oil that is kept burbling on the Cona. She fills the cup with milk and looks around.

He lowers his head, picks up the pen and begins to scrutinise the top sheet.

Let her not fasten on me, he thinks. *I could do without this.*

Then she is standing in front of him. She does not introduce herself.

'I checked it out,' she says. 'Your fucking gardener reference. It's under Botany.'

Wearily he looks at her.

'I did say.'

'You're a jerk-off,' she says. She is angry, and he notices that anger makes her interesting. There is a small red spot on her cheek, and that curl of her lips that he noticed in the lecture theatre is half-snarl half-smile.

'Look, miss,' he says. 'Why don't you sit down and we'll talk this over. I think you're missing the point.'

'What is the fucking point? That's what I want to know. When I started here, I was expecting that at least someone would have a fucking brain. Instead of that, I get fucking old farts everywhere. Boring bastards with Anglo-Saxon and Post-Modernism and all that stupid shit. I mean, what do they think it's actually about.'

'What?'

'Fucking literature, that's what. It's about something, isn't it?'

'You've lost me.' He is uncomfortably aware that she is looking down on him, that when he looks straight ahead he is facing her groin, where the elastic leggings provide him with a view of what appears to be a cleft low down in her *mons pubis*, a suggestion of another smile altogether less angry and more dangerous. The state of grace. Sweat is suddenly pungent at his armpits, between his thighs.

'Right,' she says. She puts her coffee mug down on the edge of page three of the notes, a tiny splash spreading sepia over the blue ink, a blue fizz growing on each letter. She pulls off her plastic jacket and reveals a black top ornamented with heraldic flowers and transparent in places, a black bra clearly visible under it all.

She must be so cold. How do women walk around in November with so little on? Skirts? Blouses as thin as crêpe paper, thinner sometimes. I am always cold. They metabolise more quickly, bodies burning up with fierce energy, while I am sluggish, clogged with sloth, torpid.

'Want to know why I came to college?'

He shrugs. He knows. He has heard it before five hundred times.

'You're probably thinking, working class, poor family background, wants to get ahead. Right? Dead wrong. Dead wrong about one thing. I don't give a shit about getting ahead.'

She is or is not working class? Which? No need to ask. Look at her. And the word fuck should be a give-away but is not these days.

'The reason I came here is because I was stupid enough to think that people who had brains actually used them. I expected people would talk about real things. Instead of that, it's all second hand. It's everybody else's idea of what happens, that's what the whole thing is about. It's all fucking *criticism.*'

'You should transfer to Philosophy,' he says wryly. 'They have a much better handle on reality.'

She stares at him. He takes a quick nervous gulp of coffee and feels the scald on the back of his tongue and throat. A bite of pastry fails to assuage the hurt.

'Just tell me one thing interesting,' she says. 'One thing interesting that's going to come up in the course. Or else I'm gone.'

'Look, miss, you mightn't believe it, but I don't give a shit whether you're on my course or not. My salary isn't based on having you on it.'

He can hardly believe that he has risen far enough from his torpor to be angry. He hears his own voice at a distance and is able to marvel at it, a phenomenon, a thing in itself.

'That's it so. I knew it all along.'

'What now?'

'You're just another boring fart.'

Taken aback, he smiles first.

'You don't put a tooth in it.'

'It's so fucking . . . British. Put a tooth in it. Law de daw.'

'You're just trying to get up my nose.'

'Just one thing? Just tell me one little teenshy weenshy interesting thing.' She flashes a smile at him and leans forward so that he can smell her breath, and it smells of apples and coffee, a heady mixture of open air and Nescafé, sweet and sour. The tilt accentuates her breasts, which are the only opulent part of her, full and generous, no angles. The whole thing is suddenly, unbearably erotic.

'Just one thing.'

'OK,' he says. 'One thing.' He inhales slowly, filling up with her, his head spinning on the mixture.

One thing, he thinks. I need one thing interesting.

Out of the corner of his eye, he catches a glimpse of something brown, furtive, in the scrawny plants outside the window. A small bird, or a rat scavenging. The movement unnerves him.

'The next lecture is on *The Bestiary*,' he says. '*The Physiologus*. Ever heard of it?'

He wipes a line across his forehead with the back of his hand. When he looks at it, the skin is dry. Where has the sweat gone?

He tells her about the ancient *Physiologus* – bawdy, didactic, crude in the extreme. He outlines the manuscript's history: its putative beginnings in Alexandria, transformation at the hands of early Christian scholars, translations into Ethiopian, Syriac, Arabic and Latin. The Synod of Gelasius in 496 which banned the text. She listens and drinks her coffee. At first she is remote, evaluating his performance from that distance which she has set up herself. But she is drawn in. The crowds come between lectures and go out again. The staff behind the counter change. Almost an hour passes before she interrupts. By then she is leaning forward again. Their heads are close. Her eyes are bright, her mouth hangs open a little.

'So,' she says at last, 'what's in it? Why did Gelasius ban it?'

He notices that she gets the name right. Sharp.

'That's the whole point of the lecture,' he says. 'You have to go to find out.'

'No, it isn't,' she tells him. 'The point of the lecture is a fucking reference. It's a jerk-off. It's you giving us something to do and justifying the department hanging on to you. Or have you got tenure?'

He is surprised by the question, the terms of the question.

'I'm permanent.'

'You never said a truer word,' she says. 'OK, I'll look it up.' She gets up to go.

'No, hang on a sec,' he says. 'Sit down. I'll save you the trouble of coming to the lecture.'

She sits down suspiciously.

He tells her the bestiary story of how the female elephant seduces her mate by offering him the mandrake root. He explains the moral drawn by the early Christians, that the Adam and Eve myth is refracted throughout the natural world, that the female is always dangerous.

'Do not become ensnared by carnal pleasure, or you may be slain by the devil. Wine and women easily seduce the man of God. That's the meaning of the tale. But it goes back further than the meaning, you see. The elephant and the mandrake root are primeval sex. They are the open carnal nature that the church must suppress.'

'Yeah, right,' she says. But he knows from the tone that it is not incredulity. Carnality is in the air between them, a tangible presence. He shivers at the recognition.

'Or the hyena which was said to have a stone in its eye which allows a man to see into the future if he keeps it under his tongue.'

She rocks back on her seat and stares at him. 'I'm sorry,' she says. 'I was really pissed off that time earlier. I went too far.'

He shrugs. 'It's OK. I deserve it.'

She smiles and puts a hand down on his where it holds the biro horizontally over the page. She says nothing. Her nails are painted green. The hand rests there no more than a second, but he has time to feel its bones, its sinews, the insistence of its pulse. He senses that metabolism consuming her in fractious haste. He thinks when she takes it away its imprint will be there, the lifelines and love-lines of her palm etched in negative on the back of his hand, but when she does, there is nothing left. He looks at the back of his hand and it is the same.

'Gotta run,' she says, and almost immediately she is up and headed towards the door. He shouts goodbye and she nods her head. She may have been saying hello to someone on the way down, he is not sure.

She didn't come to the next lecture, and although I laid my wares out much as I had done for her that day in the restaurant, no other student seemed so taken by *The Physiologus.* I checked afterwards, and the three texts I recommended were not disturbed in their dusty stack. Two weeks later, she was there again, sitting halfway up the steps, a red jacket and blue shoes. I could see the shoes because she sat in an aisle seat, twisted sideways, one foot cocked out over the steps.

I was talking about animals with reference to the bestiaries and the collection and advertisement of freaks, and she had a notepad and a biro and occasionally put in furious bursts of writing. In between, she chewed the pen top with a look of intense concentration.

'The composers of bestiaries projected their own obsessions on to the animals they described,' I was saying. 'As a consequence, the bestiary is a good indicator of what was considered taboo, or simply bad form. The underlying agenda of the Holy Mother Church is everywhere, of course, especially the sexual one. Sex and dirt. Sex and shit.'

That was for the nuns. And for her.

I had noted this trend in my lecturing – the crudity, the urge to shock, delight in offending the prurient. Lecture after lecture nowadays, no matter how I swore to be clean-mouthed.

I had time to wonder how my course had taken this scatological turn. I saw the pile of manila folders that constituted my notes for the same course, delivered last year and completely different, sanitary and safe, stacked untouched on the floor beside my desk. The new ones, piled high, scribbled all over, tumbling with ideas. Not for the first time the thought struck me that I was on the verge of the greatest discovery of my life, that the prodding and shocking was all part of an inexorable progress towards an over-whelming truth. The existence of this truth, a shimmering form on the edge of consciousness, drove me on, at the same time a jus-tification for the grossness and the imagined object of it.

So I told them about the weasel which was held to be a dis-gusting animal as a consequence of the female's habit of receiv-ing sperm into her mouth. How she delivered her young through her ear.

How it was forbidden to eat weasels.

How the viper inserted his head into the mouth of the female and ejaculated down her throat. In her carnal ecstasy the female bit off the head of her mate.

How it was forbidden to eat vipers lest the practice become current among Christians.

How hyenas were reviled because they changed sex annual-ly, clearly unacceptable in the Judaeo-Christian tradition, and imitated the sound of vomiting in order to attract Good Samar-itans whom they ate. Given the injunction to visit the sick, I suggested, churchmen could not be expected to approve of such practices.

There was more in that vein, delivered to a tittering audi-ence. I finished on excrement and urine, and a flourish of Sir Thomas Browne on toads.

'Finally, as a coda to all of this, let me quote Browne – see last week's lecture for the reference – on the question of whether, as he so succinctly put it, "a Toad properly pisseth, that is dis-tinctly and separately voideth the serious excretions."

I took a deep breath, checked that I did in fact have the quotation written out, and was about to deliver Sir Thomas's admirably crude estimate of the answer when I heard someone say, 'Excuse me.'

I looked up and she was half-propped on her seat, elevated but not standing, one hand in the air. Her fingernails were red.

'A question no less,' I said weakly. 'Just what I've been waiting for.'

'What I was wondering is, is this stuff about piss and shit meant to shock us, or is there going to be a question on it or something?'

I saw the nuns nodding their heads to each other. Everybody else tittered again. I felt my bowels freeze suddenly, something down there in spasm, the urgent need to go to the gents.

'Both,' I said and smiled. I was hoping the smile was disarming.

'OK,' she said. 'Well, I'm not shocked, so it's a fail on that point. I checked up on the Tradescants, and nearly everything in their collection was authentic, botanical stuff. You just threw that in because they were gardeners by profession and you thought it would piss us off, which I find objectionable. Most of the stuff you're talking about now is covered in a book called *Beasts and Bawdy*, by Ann Clark, published by Dent. I have the reference and it's in the library. So, what's the point?'

'Actually, that is the point.'

I was playing for time. I was lost. And I was listening to a tiny sound coming from behind me, behind the wooden panelling at my back. They have rats here, too, I thought. The country is full of them.

'What, actually?'

'That you checked the reference.'

'That,' she said, 'is fatuous in the extreme. If I wanted to learn about a fucking library, I'd have got a job in one.'

The theatre erupted. Louts hooted, nuns chuckled, the can-dos and the teachers haw-hawed and elbowed each other. I was defeated.

When the noise died down, I waved my hands and smiled, aware that there was something desperate in my smile, and said, 'All right, ladies and gentlemen, after that devastating critique, I'll call it a day. Next week we'll be coming up to date a little. We'll deal with the unicorn and the maiden and the self-destructive habits of beavers, who castrate themselves when they are trapped by hunters.'

The theatre emptied quickly and by the time I had shuffled my notes into my briefcase she was gone.

I don't know what happened to the rest of the afternoon, but at five thirty I found myself in the college bookshop. I was buying her a copy of Ted Hughes's *Crow*. And I was crying.

He has conceived the notion that she is hiding somewhere on the campus, and so he rushes blindly from student bar to common room. He trawls the hide-holes: the shaded seats of the President's Garden; the pond; the social areas; the library. She is not there. He waits for the turn of the hour and watches people spilling from lectures. It comes into his head that she told him she was doing classical studies, and so he follows students to a room where a patrician foreigner lectures on Stoicism and Seneca. He does not recognise the man.

He leaves the lecture and comes out into the cold evening air. He is aware of panic growing like an animal in his gut. How could she do it to him? He remembers how he laid out the story of *The Physiologus* for her, trying to make it interesting, trying to make her feel she was not wasting her time. It was an invitation:

this is my world. She could have looked at it and understood because everything was there: the scholarship, the loneliness, desire. She had responded by humiliating him.

It is a sharp November night, full of woodsmoke and crystal stars. He sits on the bench opposite the Student Common Room and tries to calm himself. After a time he notices that he is shivering.

He remembers her thin face peaking at a sharp nose, her thinness in the elastic clothing, the energy emanating from the touch of her hand.

By an effort of will he imagines her sitting in the second chair in his study, the one he reserved years ago, when he was made permanent, for the partner who never materialised, sipping a sherry and listening to his next article. He imagines her making small criticisms. The domestic image warms him for a time.

Then he remembers that the heating oil is gone, that the house has been cold for four days, and that he has been heating the kitchen from the gas oven. That he is sleeping with coats on the bed. And then there are the noises, the rats, the conversations. It is as though the house has somehow retained the imprint of previous occupants human and animal. A spasm of self-pity overtakes him. When he looks at his watch, he knows yet again that the heating-oil company will be closed. Friday night, another weekend plunging into the chaos of his private life, the emptiness.

When he made his way to the bookshop, he was already half-paralysed by dread. He stood inside the door for a time, checking through the recent arrivals, but really just allowing the heat to soak through him. Then the thought came to him that he should buy her the book, Hughes's bleak look at the animal of the world, the survivor.

She wore black, too. A crow perched in his memory.

'Closing time, sir,' the girl said.

'Yes, yes,' he said.

'Are you all right, sir?'

He looked blankly at her.

'Are you OK? Would you like a glass of water?'

He handed her the book and fished in his pocket for the money. A spill of banknotes littered the floor, the table. The shop girl gasped. Another girl rushed over and began to pick them up, brown and blue and green rags rustling in their hands. Their heads together at the level of his knees.

They were both redheads.

What were the odds? Important to calculate, if only he knew how. Somewhere there would be statistics. There was no such thing as a random occurrence. No accidents. The girl could be anywhere. She might never come back again. Or she might. Which was worse?

'There must be five hundred quid,' the shop girl said.

'Jesus.'

He saw that there was burnt food oozing from the door of the cooker and a rubble of crumbs and pieces of food: utensils, a mug, tea bags and paper on the worktop. How long had this been accumulating? He wandered around the house, small enough not to need much time, and saw that the only room that was habitable was his study, what had originally been the third, tiny bedroom. Here everything was neat: the wall of books catalogued according to the Dewey system; the desk with his notes to one side, a small stack of books he had been meaning to read on the other, pen and paper in the centre; the chair angled to the desk the way he liked it. He saw it all suddenly in metaphoric terms. The study was the empty formality of his lectures, the pointlessness of his academic work. The rest of the house was the filth and chaos of his private life. Somehow, he knew, the lectures he had been giving recently were the objective expression of whatever it was that was destroying him. He even wondered whether the girl in the black leggings was a creation of a disordered mind, the scrambled expression of his despair.

'Get a grip on yourself,' he said aloud. 'You're falling.'

He listened to the word for a minute, hearing it prolonged in the air like the resonance of a musical chord. Where was he falling? What was he falling into?

His seventh lecture was on disease. He had forgotten his notes, the leather bag empty and caved-in looking. He stood at the podium, swaying a little, swallowing frequently. He looked about him but could not see her. He closed his eyes and began to speak.

'Pliny,' he said, and then recollected that he was supposed to have moved on, that he was supposed to have come up to the sixteenth century at least. Where had he been at the last lesson? Was it Sir Thomas Browne?

'Pliny is a little outside our field of reference for today,' he said. 'But it should be said that he was a firm believer in crickets as a cure for earache. Perhaps, anyone with a hangover might like to look up the reference. There's a perfectly good prescription in it, and it's not a controlled drug. First you catch your cricket using an ant tied to a hair . . .'

There was laughter. He had them again. He felt the air cool suddenly, as though someone had opened a door. He remembered the fury of cleaning he had gone through on Sunday night, a kind of purge. The whole house smelled of disinfectant and Toilet Duck still. This was Tuesday. Or was it Friday? Pliny also favoured the seminal fluid of a boar collected from the sow as it dripped. Mustn't say that. Offensive. Trying to offend again – where does the urge come from?

'*The Anatomy of Melancholy*,' he said. 'Robert Burton, remember? Hamlet? You'll have come across that gentleman in Professor Dawkins's course? Burton says . . .'

He felt unsteady on his feet, uncertain suddenly of the provenance of the quotation he was about to recite. Where did it come from? He was unaware that it was there, crouched in his memory. Was it complete? Would it emerge whole and live in his mind and theirs, or was it to be stillborn?

'*The devil*, Burton says, *being a slender incomprehensible spirit, can easily insinuate and wind himself into human bodies, and cunningly couched in our bowels, vitiate our healths, terrify our souls with fearful dreams, and shake our mind with furies.*'

Terrify our souls with fearful dreams. Last night he had dreamed of the girl in the black leggings. He saw her first in her natural shape, the thin face, the shape of her pelvic bones in the elastic fabric. She was very close to him, her face close, and he could smell her breath, her apple-and-coffee air between them. And then she was animal. There was hair on her face and her features had elongated. She opened her mouth and took his penis into it, and he ejaculated spontaneously. He looked down and saw her eyes open, ecstatic, the pupils enlarging like saucers. Then she bit down hard, and there was blood flowing as copiously as his semen, spurting with the same spasm. Then he was awake and he could not account for the pain in his groin, although the sticky wet of his shorts was plain enough. He lay doubled on his side, clutching his testicles for ten minutes, and when it eased, he got up and showered.

He was conscious suddenly of a great pressure of thoughts and words, voices even, crowding his mind, clamouring to be uttered. The words seemed too fast to be spoken. Confusion. Babble. Then Topsell's clear confident prose coughed itself into his mouth and he spoke it as though it was his own. '*To provoke urine when a man's yard is stopt . . .*'

It was pouring out of him now, a torrent of filth. He knew not whence it came, was powerless to stop it. Somewhere in the bleakness of his unconscious he had secreted it, awaiting the propitious time. He felt the importance of the hour, the timely presence of exactly the right words. His voice settled into a chant, sing-song, like a self-conscious poet.

'To provoke urine when a man's yard is stopt, there is nothing so excellent as the dung or filth which proceedeth from the urine which a horse hath made, being mingled with wine and afterwards strained and poured into the nostrils of the party vexed. Topsell's *History of Foure-Footed Beasts.*'

People were leaving. Through the diaphanous filter of his eyelids, he saw their shadows mounting the steps and spilling out through the swing-doors. Nun-shapes, abandoning him finally. Others sat on, open-mouthed or laughing openly.

'Urine was also believed to cure ulcers and afflictions of the anus. *Take the sweat of a horse admixed with urine and it will cure the belly-ache, the belly-worm and the serpent of the belly. Sirius rising, collect the urine of an ass for leprosy . . .*'

He opened his eyes suddenly, alerted by the silence. She was there, the only one left in the fifth row, staring at him. He stared back. There was a burning pain behind his eyes.

'Gangrene of the hands, feet, eyeballs and genitals,' he told her quietly, 'is reported by Thucydides in 430 BC.'

He looked around and saw that there was a chair standing against the wall behind his back. He slumped into it. His face was wet.

She came down the steps and knelt down in front of him.

'You're not well,' she said. Fifteen, maybe twenty people held their breath, watching the comedy. Even the louts were gone. The nuns were gone. Most of the teachers were gone. The people left were mostly girls.

'No,' he said.

'Where do you live? I'm taking you home.'

'No,' he said. 'Filthy. The house is in no condition. No visitors.'

She took his hand and helped him to his feet, led him slowly up the steps and out on to the landing. A small swarm of his students buzzed at the end of the corridor. They fell silent when he came out. He was conscious of their gaze, a kind of awe in it.

'I bought you a present,' he told her.

He opened his bag. Then he remembered the chaos of bank-notes on the floor, the shop girls fussing over him. He saw the book sitting on the counter to the left of the cash register, the pattern it made with the notes, the rectangles curiously echoing each other. Both shop girls were redheads. The foreigner was talking about Seneca. Thomas Carew addressed a strumpet and concluded that she had once been in a state of grace.

'I forgot,' he said. 'I didn't buy it because it was vulgar.' He wanted to tell her about the signs, but he knew she would be suspicious. *Hasten slowly*, he told himself. *Trust no one.*

She walked him the quarter mile to his house, found his key in the pocket of his jacket and let him in. The smell – Parazone, ammonia, Jeyes Fluid, furniture polish, fly-spray – was over-powering.

'Jesus,' she said. 'This place is fucking poisonous.'

She sat him in a kitchen chair and went round opening all the windows. He stared bleakly at the cooker. In all his cleaning he had missed the encrusted edges of the doors. Something black had oozed out at the lower edge, a bevelled lava which here and there had dripped onto the floor. A dead fly swam in still life, like a prehistoric insect trapped in amber.

'What's your name?'

'Vanessa,' she said, rolling up her sleeves. Where the elastic pinched her forearm reminded him of his first dream, the leggings nicking her thighs. He groaned.

Vanessa, the ignorance is so great. Thousands of years of it. What have we known in that time? Between Galen and Harvey there is nothing but the same invincible ignorance.

The reproductive system of hares. That innocent creature.

That he had two reproductive systems.

That his pizzle was directed backwards.

That he pissed backwards and copulated backwards.

That the female hare could carry a child and get a child at the same time. For the Matrix is yet another animal within us and which is not subjected unto the law of our will.

And snakes. They said that snakes grew of their own volition from the spinal column of dead men.

I feel the burden of it. It is in my head, it has penetrated my cells. I feel I am sweating it.

When you took me home that night I thought you could save me. I thought I was going mad. I said, 'Stay with me, Vanessa,' because by then you had given me your name. You said, 'No way.' I wanted to tell you that it was all for you, all the words, all the ideas. That I was inarticulate was because of you. Not that I could stop talking. But to talk and articulate are not the same.

He sits there, watching her move. He sees in her the lineaments of the animal. She arches her foot when she walks. Her knees bend slightly, elasticity in everything. When she leans over, he sees the cleft of her buttocks, a seam in the centre which is not in the cloth. Her scut is there.

'Vanessa.'

When he begins to talk, she is frightened. Her fear makes her face white, dark pools for her eyes.

She is frightened. 'Let the hare sit,' someone said.

'If I could stop, I would.'

There is a flow to this, a swollen flood.

Bees, they never lapse into love nor bear young by the pangs of childbirth. Virgil, *Georgics.* She is too cold.

'Vanessa, save me.'

'Got to go now,' she says.

'Vanessa, stay with me.'

'Got to go.'

Fear in her eyes.

He watches her go out. He shivers although the room has warmed. Then he gets out of the chair and picks up his coat. He puts his coat on, counting aloud to sixty. He goes to the door and looks out. He hears her footsteps but does not see her. He closes the door quietly and steps out into the streetlight. He sees her turn the corner far ahead of him. He follows her.

Virgil's voice in my head, lines learned in childhood. *The Aeneid.* Terrible O Queen are the sorrows you command me to revive. *Infandum reginæ iubes renovare dolorem.* How little Latin he has been required to remember. She turns left and is walking along College Avenue. He slows, lightens his steps, hugs the shadows. He studies her gait. She rolls along now, unburdened. No voices in her head, the weight of the past, a thousand years of scholarship in ignorance.

'Don't think of it,' he says, and a girl passing, a secretary or a shop girl on her way home from work, stares at him.

'Fuck you, too,' he says, and she hurries on.

Three streets further and they are into flatland. The tenements are high, fourth or fifth storeys clawing for light over the rooftops of neighbours. Gardens are dead hydrangeas or overgrown bony fuchsia. There are broken windows patched with cardboard. A piece of paper hangs on a cast-iron door knocker: *Mick gone down to Waxy's for a pint meet me there.* There are broken iron railings and gates that have fallen on their hinges and stick half-open. A small smear of vomit against a door.

She comes at last to the corner house on the street. She takes a key from the pocket of her jacket and stands under the street lamp selecting the right one. Then she puts the key in the lock and disappears inside without looking up or down. He stands under the same street light until he sees a light go on three floors up. When she comes to pull the curtains, he hurries away.

'They're offering me leave,' he tells the woman on his left. 'On condition I seek medical help. That's why I'm here. Leave, until the end of term, extension through Michaelmas term if I need it. The prof says I'm too valuable. Can you believe that? My course? Valuable.'

The woman says that she is sure it is valuable.

'Like hell. He's just covering himself. Unfair dismissal, that's what he thinks is valuable. Statutory sick leave et cetera. You can't fire someone for being sick.'

The woman says she should think not.

'No fucking way,' he says. He is feeling excited. He feels he has taken up a cause. For the first time in days there are no voices, driven out by this new commitment.

The woman shuffles in her chair, managing to put a little space between herself and him and says yes there is no way.

'Not even if you're sick in the head.'

'No, not even then. Although maybe if it came against the work. That kind of thing can come against the work. Not like being handicapped.'

'You're right,' he says. 'That's why I'm not taking this sabbatical. I'm going to turn up every day. On time. They can fire you for unpunctuality, did you know that? Oh yes, that's how they do it. It's all in the detail, the minutiæ. You have to watch out for the minutiæ.'

The woman says she always watches out for it.

'They get you every time.'

'Nasty things.'

'Your turn,' he tells the woman when the nurse comes out. 'Make him give you a prescription, otherwise it's just a waste of a visit.'

But when his turn comes, he speaks about headaches, not voices. He saw instantly that the doctor was in the pay of the university, foolish enough even to display his medical degrees on the walls.

He never mentions the sounds or the voices or his new ability to watch himself from outside.

The doctor peers into his eyes with a light-pen.

After a time, Tom says, 'Do you mind.'

'I beg your pardon?'

Tom says, 'I've had enough of this.'

A thousand years of stupidity and then, in the blink of an eye, they invent a machine that sees into the mind. A simple pen.

'I'm checking for abnormalities. Behind the eye.'

'Just give me the fucking prescription,' he says.

Behind the eye is my brain. If he could see in there he would read: KEEP OUT NO TRESPASSING.

The doctor backs off. He sits for a moment on the edge of a desk and then stands up again. A nervous man.

'You need something to calm you down,' Tom says.

The doctor laughs uncomfortably. 'No need for that,' he says. 'You just took me by surprise.'

'What about the prescription?'

'Which prescription had you in mind?'

Another trap. Name the specific and you name the disease.

'That's your job,' he says.

Ants are no good. Piss. Pig spunk. Suddenly he is aware of the inadequacy of his scholarship. He cannot recall one thing to make good the broken mind. There is no specific against a fracture in the bond between the world and the way of seeing it. The realisation is a loss of innocence. Tears begin to roll.

'I am going mad,' he tells the doctor. 'I know it.'

The doctor says, 'Now, now. It's not that bad.' He rips three large tissues from a box on his couch and hands them out. 'Here,' he says.

'I have to go.'

'Take your time,' the doctor says, but he stands up and opens the door quickly. 'Come back when you feel able to talk about it.'

There are different women in the waiting room. They stare up at him. He wants to tell them to be careful, to watch out for trick questions, not to let him look into them, but the voices have begun again. The pressure from inside is enormous. He feels he is going to crack open like an egg dropped suddenly into boiling water, the yoke and white burbling out at the fissure, revealing everything.

He stands at a bus stop and tells no one that a spermatical

emission equivalent to one drachm is equivalent unto the effusion of sixty ounces of blood and therefore we cannot but think it abridgeth our days. And although he holds his tongue and never utters a sound, the three elderly women stare at him, and a young man with long hair tied back in a ponytail moves away to the other side of the stop and watches resolutely in the direction from which the bus will not come.

He has £575 in his pocket, and when he takes out the wad of notes, the driver coughs into his hand. He gives him a note and gets the right change. When he sits down, he sees the driver watching him in the high convex mirror that allows him to see back along the bus. He notices that the driver is misshapen, grossly enlarged at the top. His eyes bulge like a toad's.

He has been careful to bring the correct papers this time. He stands at the podium in front of a packed lecture theatre. There are students everywhere: sitting in the aisles; sitting cross-legged on the floor in the right-hand corner; standing at the back behind the louts. There is an air of expectancy. He sees that at last the penny has dropped. Ten years.

He begins by saying that the intrinsic value of metaphor is something which should not be underestimated. In mathematics, for example, there are things which cannot be understood except in terms of imagery. He instances fractal geometry, where the constructed image is acknowledged to be no more than an approximation of the reality it attempts to describe.

He smiles. Nobody smiles back.

She is there, too. In her usual seat. He leans forward and adopts a conspiratorial air.

'I could tell you things,' he says.

He talks about the recent death of a lecturer in Physics. He tells them about the research the man was doing.

'The Theory of Everything. That's what the physicists are after. The Holy Grail they call it. Of course, they couldn't let him get away with it. He got too close.'

He winks broadly and jerks his thumb in the direction of the ceiling.

'They got to him, of course. It goes without saying. All of us are under threat. Constant threat.'

He is wearing a jacket and tie for the first time in anybody's memory, a neatly pressed shirt, a trousers with creases. He stands up straight now, almost a military posture, hands firmly at his sides.

'Anybody who got even close would understand everything. He would know about everything. Think about it. The power.'

He coughs.

A colleague has just pushed in past the crush of louts at the door. He stands at the back, arms folded.

'We must be circumspect. So . . . to get back to the matter in hand, and stand by for further updates.'

He takes up his lecture notes and reads carefully:

'A man emigrates from Kerry circa 1965 – the date isn't important. This man gets a job on a building site in London.'

He looks up bleakly.

'McAlpine is the company,' he says. He waits for the nuns to write it down.

'The job he gets is night watchman. He's worried about being up all night because in Kerry he never did stay up late because his mammy wouldn't let him. He asks the lads on the site what he should do. "Oh, bejaze," says one of them, "you'll need a thermos flask." "What's that?" The Kerryman asks. They explain to him the multitudinous advantages of thermos flasks, the hot tay in the middle of the night, mushroom soup if you wanted it, et cetera. The Kerryman says he'll get one and could they say the name again for him. "I'll do better than that," says one of the lads. "I'll write it down for you." He takes a pencil from behind his ear, because he is an apprentice carpenter, and tears a scrap of paper from his *Daily Mirror*, because he votes Labour. He writes: condom.'

There is a rumble of expectation from the crowd. 'This is a good one now,' he hears someone say. He smiles up at them. The colleague is frowning.

'So he takes the chit of paper to a chemist shop that the lads have pointed out to him. He goes up to the nice girl at the counter and hands her the note. "What size?" she says. "Large, medium or small?"'

He pauses and draws a deep breath through his nose. He has them, he sees that. Why didn't he try this approach years ago? He screws up his eyes and makes an effort of recognition. It comes to him that the colleague is Charlie Kennedy. Semi-permanent? Temporary whole-time? One step down.

'"Well," says the Kerryman. "I'll be on the job all night so I'll need wan that'll hold about three pints."'

In the uproar he sees the girl, Vanessa, gathering her things. She mustn't leave, he knows. She mustn't leave before the end of the lecture because he must speak to her. He signals wildly for the laughter to stop.

'I could tell you things,' he shouts and the crowd falls silent. 'I could tell you things.' She sits back down and looks at her fingernails. He sees that they are painted blue.

'There are spies everywhere, for example.'

He looks up at them, all his confidence gone.

'A thousand years of invincible ignorance and in the blink of an eye we can see inside someone's brain? What kind of a species behaves like that? What have we done to ourselves? We who have gathered the semen of hogs. Who have torn the eye from the hyena for the invisible stone. Who have traduced the harmless hare and accused him of the most bestial acts that we ourselves have practised? Never think, never think we could not have understood everything a thousand, two thousand years ago. That is the message. All this was not accidental. We are to blame.'

He was shouting. 'We are to blame!' The theatre was deathly silent. Charlie Kennedy stared open-mouthed.

'We are culpable in this as in all things,' he shouts. 'I know this. I know it. Don't ask me how. *Infandum regina iubes renovare dolorem.*

'If you sleep with me,' he says looking directly at the girl, 'the people who are violating my head will go away. They could not bear your innocence, your state of grace.'

The crowd gasps. The girl stands up very suddenly and rushes upwards, stumbling on the central aisle. People on the steps move their feet and crush in close to the seats. Along the back, the louts lean closer to the wall and watch her as she passes. Charlie Kennedy attempts to stop her, a look of concern on his face, and then changes his mind and steps aside. She goes out through the swing-doors with a bang.

'Open the temple gates unto my love,' he recites, his hands at his side, his head thrown back. He is looking up at the roof. 'Open them wide that she may enter in, and all the postes adorne as doth behove and all the pillours deck with garlands trim.'

And then when the door clatters shut he shouts: 'It was suicide! The bastards forced him to commit suicide because he had found the Theory of Everything.'

Charlie Kennedy has a hand on his arm. 'Take it easy, Tom,' he is saying. His voice is soothing and concerned, but there is a gleam in his eye, sharp as a serpent's tooth. *I know that gleam. It is triumph. The bastard is crazy, he thinks. That's another one gone, another step on the ladder. But I have tenure. Not everyone has tenure here.*

'Tom, Tom, slow down.'

He strides towards the door, ignoring Charlie Kennedy's hand, ignoring what he says. Some of his notes slip from the cardboard folder and spill onto the floor. He stops abruptly and stares at the pattern they make. He tilts his head to one side as he looks.

'What is it, Tom?' Charlie Kennedy says.

He shakes his head. 'Meaningless,' he says. 'Nothing there.' He turns and goes through the door. 'I mustn't lose her,' he says.

'Tom, leave that girl be,' Charlie Kennedy says. 'It isn't right.'

He knows where she is going. He hardly needs to keep his eyes open. He walks along the edge of the footpath, curious about the sense of elation that has overtaken him. He thinks about it, examines it as a thing in itself. He sees himself turning his elation this way and that, like an *objet d'art*, checking its provenance, checking for flaws, for imperfections, for the mark of the maker. He concludes that it is indeed a flawless thing, perfect in itself, something to be joyed in.

It's a perfect day, he thinks. That's why I'm happy. And I have declared myself. Two truths are told as prologue to the swelling act. I told her I loved her and I have given out the secret. Now they know that I know. They know that all my years of scholarship have not been for nothing.

He whistles as he walks. He balances on the exact edge of the footpath, his arms extended from his sides like a tightrope walker. Then he begins to dodge the lines on the pavement, stepping only on the unmarked places. He is so absorbed that he does not notice her standing at the door of her house, watching him.

'Leave me alone,' she says.

He shakes his head. 'I love you.'

'No, you fucking don't, you mad bastard.'

'You can't drive me away. I know why you're doing this.'

'You know nothing.'

'You're wrong,' he says. 'I have read widely. But I have terrible dreams. Remember Burton? He had them, too, I'm convinced.'

'*The Anatomy of Melancholy*,' she says suddenly. It is as though a light has come on in her head. She looks at him differently, as though studying him really for the first time. 'Come inside. I'll get you a cup of tea. Then we're going to have to call someone. I'm not fucking nursemaiding you.'

They go up the grimy stairs. His hand slides on the banister and he feels the years of chip fat on the paint, the slime of a thousand students' sweat. The carpet is so worn that the bare boards show through in foot-sized pieces. A board is missing on the first landing, and in the darkness below he sees cigarette butts, tissue paper, chewing gum.

'For Christ's sake, come on,' she says, catching his arm and pulling him away from the hole.

'Everything is important,' he says, by way of explanation. 'Everything. Most importantly what is discarded. Or appears to be.'

Her flat is one room. An untidy bed in one corner. A two-burner Camping Gaz stove on a Formica table, an obscene red rubber tube linking the stove to the scarred blue bottle beneath. A sink. Two chairs and another table by the window. The view is of the concrete garden of the house behind.

She fills a kettle and lights the gas. He sits by the window and sees a clothesline down in the shadows, small things swinging in the cold.

'You're not well.' She is kinder now. When she turns, he can see that she is concerned.

'I am not,' he says.

'You should go for help.'

He shrugs. 'What can I do? It's too dangerous.'

'No,' she says, 'that's all in your head. That's just what you think now. If you had help, you'd see things differently.'

He looks up at her.

'I feel like a puppy,' he says, 'begging from his mistress for a scrap.'

She folds her arms and leans back against the table with the kettle on it. He has the strange feeling that her body is humming.

'You have to stop saying all those things.'

'I can't. They're in my head. They just come out. Sometimes I don't even think them. Somehow they just . . . appear. My skull utters them but my brain hasn't formed them. Like that.'

She makes the tea and they sit close at the table, husbanding the heat between them, the steam rising in a shaft of bleak sunlight that comes down the valley in the rooftop behind. In the end she sighs and says, 'I can't do anything for you.'

'I know that,' he says. 'I see that.'

'Not for the reasons you think.'

'No. Of course not.'

He says he knows she cannot love him, not after what he has said and done. The enormity of it overwhelms him. He puts the cup down on the floor to use both of his hands. He gestures towards the sky. 'I've gone too far,' he says. 'The things I've done and seen.'

She shakes her head. 'It's not that,' she insists. His foot disturbs the cup and it tips over on to its side, the last of the tea spilling out. They watch it spread into the groove of the floorboards. Then she picks up the cup and stands it on the table out of his reach.

'I have a baby.'

He looks around.

'Yes,' she says. 'Here. A friend minds him while I'm at lectures. That's why I'm hardly ever around. I can't bear to leave him for long. That's why I was so angry about all those references. I spent hours in the library looking them up because I thought they were important. I hated you for taking me away from him. I understand now.'

He begins to cry.

'I'm so sorry,' he says.

'It's real for you, isn't it? Not like the others.' She hands him a tissue from her sleeve. It is folded into a neat square. He wipes his eyes, but the water continues to flow silently.

'He's six months old today.'

'Is there a father?'

'Of course there's a fucking father,' she says. 'You don't think I did it in vitro.'

He shakes his head. 'I meant here.'

She shakes her head. 'Fucked off straight away,' she says. 'Good riddance.'

He says he could help. He has money. He has not spent his salary in over a year. His house is full of banknotes. He will give them all to her so she can get a bigger flat.

'In fact,' he says, a sly look coming into his eyes, 'why don't you move into my house? I'll sublet a room to you. It'd be a purely commercial arrangement.'

She laughs. 'I'm sure it would.'

'You'll do it?'

She says no, she won't do it.

He gets up and walks around, rubbing his palms together. He says that she will regret it. His house is comfortable, three bedrooms, a kitchen, a full bathroom and shower, central heating.

He's almost never at home because of his researches. He slaps his palms together and his pacing speeds up. He tells her that she is beautiful but that beauty is dangerous. She has power and she must use the power magnanimously. She must yield to him. If he can lie with her and spill his seed into her, it will cure his mind. An emission of semen equivalent to one drachm, he tells her, is all that is required. That will relieve the pressure behind his eyes because it thins the blood.

She stands up and goes behind the table. She looks around but sees only his empty mug. She picks that up.

'My baby will be home in a few minutes,' she says.

Hah! Heard it before. There is nothing new under the sun.

But just then there is a knock at the door. She rushes to it and throws it open. A red pram is pushed in and a girl follows it. The girl is older than her, more settled looking.

'Safe and sound,' the girl says. 'Changed, fed and burped. All ready for his mammy. Hello,' she says to Tom. She looks at Vanessa, one eyebrow lifted, the ghost of a leer on her face.

'This is one of my lecturers,' Vanessa says. 'Tom Ryan. He's just going.'

He shakes his head.

'Oh yes, you are,' she says.

He sees that the strange girl and Vanessa are aligned against him. They stand and glare. He smiles.

'I see the way it is,' he says. He brushes past them and goes down the stairs two at a time.

He makes elaborate preparations. First he tracks down all the banknotes. He has a shoebox that says Nike Air on the side. He jams the notes into it, squeezing the last few into awkward corners. Then he tapes up the box, running the tape along the edges to make it neat, to seal it down well. He tapes all the corners, too, and finally hefts it in his hand. Then he covers the box in brown paper and writes her address on the outside, Vanessa, 18 Boyle Street. He knows he could trace her surname at the department but feels it might compromise her, leave her exposed. He does not think he should give anything away.

From time to time, as he packs the money, he stops to listen, tilting his head slightly. Always when he does this, there is a puzzled look on his face. The voices are silent. He listens for them but they do not come.

Now he scours the kitchen again, cleaning everything. He goes around the house cleaning every surface he might have touched. *No prints*, he tells himself. *They will find nothing*. Then he unplugs the washing machine and cuts the cable at the machine end. He separates the three wires and pares them to expose the copper. He cuts away the earth. Then he winds the wire around itself and puts it in his briefcase.

'I want to tell you what has been happening,' he says. He looks up at the tiers and sees Dawkins and Lennon and Charlie Kennedy up there, sitting together at the back. They are staring impassively at the blackboard behind him. On the blackboard he has written 'FORGIVENESS TIME'. He wonders if any of them knows that it is a quotation from a Berryman poem. Also I love him, me he's done no wrong for going on fifty years. Forgiveness time. Probably not. He shuffles his lecture notes and looks down at his own neat script. After this, he thinks, I'm going to buy a computer.

'Pliny,' he says. 'Pliny spoke to me. And our old friend Sir Thomas Browne. Galen. There's an interesting man. I knew him.'

Once again he senses the order and discipline of what he is saying. It seems to him that his words have an intense clarity, like a single intense pinprick of light shining in a deserted landscape.

'Suicide is not a sin. I have it on no less an authority than Seneca.'

There is an audible gasp. Professor Dawkins shuffles uncomfortably and says something to Charlie Kennedy. Kennedy nods and looks at his watch.

'But they have all gone. That is what I wanted to explain. The voices are silent. Can you imagine what that is like? If I say to you that I have had knowledge, you will know what I mean. *Knowledge*. Because you have heard me speak about it. You know my insights. Twenty years of scholarship prepared me for it. A difficult path to follow. Now I am desolate. The voices, the power, the knowledge that I was at the centre. How can I live without it?'

They see him open his briefcase and look in. Some of them lean forward in their seats in the hope of looking into the mouth of the case.

'Come down, Vanessa. Vanessa understands everything. She is an initiate. Come down, Vanessa.'

There are hisses of 'Don't go down, Vanessa' and 'Go down, Vanessa'. A girl sitting near her reaches across two companions and tugs her arm. She says, 'He's crazy, Vanessa.'

Vanessa shakes off the hand and stands out into the aisle. Professor Dawkins stands up, too, and begins to make his way past the gaping students who sit between him and the aisle. Charlie Kennedy follows.

Professor Dawkins says, 'Stay where you are, young lady.'

Vanessa comes down as far as the second step, no further. He remembers she spoke to him from that step, the first time, the very first time. Significant.

'I sent you the money,' he says. 'You'll be all right now.' He looks up at the crowd. 'Vanessa had my baby,' he says. They stare bleakly down at him. Vanessa shakes her head. 'We did the deed of darkness in her bed. The beast with two backs.' He laughs loudly, throwing his head back a little, letting the muscles in his throat open, a full-throated laugh, a relief. 'Othello. Iago said it – the beast with two backs. We did. I gave her a baby; now I'm giving her the truth. Come closer, Vanessa.'

'Stay where you are,' Professor Dawkins shouts.

He smiles.

'I won't hurt you.'

Charlie Kennedy climbs over the back of his tier and walks along the tops of the benches. He mounts higher until he is at the back row. The louts standing there part for him and he drops to the aisle. He hurries out and the door slams behind him.

'Too late for security,' he says. He laughs. This is the truth.

He looks down at his notes and realises that after all the order is not there. The letters are random, higgledy-piggledy. He sees individual words. Hog. Slime. Heartsease. Panacea. And names. Pliny the Elder. Aristotle. Burton. He puts his finger down to steady the words and he follows the finger down to the page. If he reads exactly what he has written, he knows, the lecture will return to order. He is aware that there is water on his cheeks. He begins to read.

'God has given you one face,' he says. He notices that it is not what is on the page in front of him, that the words come from somewhere else. 'And you make yourself another. You jig, you amble and you lisp and nickname God's creatures and make your wantonness your ignorance.'

He looks up and sees that a security guard is standing at the top of the hall talking into a radio. Charlie Kennedy is beside him.

'I have tenure here,' he shouts. 'You can't get rid of me as easily as that. You bastards.'

Vanessa says, 'Take it easy, Tom.'

'You said I was lying. You left the baby on his own. What kind of a mother is that? You were trying to check up on me.'

'No,' she says. 'No, someone looked after him.'

'Remember one thing,' he says. 'I know. I *know*.

'*O rose thou art sick,*' he chants, trying to channel the loudest voice, good old William Blake the ranter, coming in loud and clear over the others. '*The invisible worm that flies in the night in the howling storm has found out thy bed of crimson joy and his dark secret love doth thy life destroy.* That's your sex. Remember *The Physiologus,* The Bestiary. I have the stone from the hyena's eye. I *have* it.' He stares into her eyes. He puts his index finger to his temple and moves it slowly through the air until it is pointing directly at her. 'It is real.'

'Fuck you,' she shouts. 'Who gives you the right?'

'Don't,' Dawkins calls to her. 'Don't say anything. Don't provoke him.' Dawkins's hands are shaking and his jelly-roll face is glistening with sweat.

'You're a bastard,' she shouts. 'You're a sadistic bastard, that's all you are. You and your fucking references. And your fucking failure rate.' Her face is white and her hands, too, are trembling. He sees that her fingernails are painted black. They are gleaming beetles at the ends of her fingers. When her hands move, the beetles ripple.

'Jesus Christ,' he says. 'They were right. Everything is corrupt.'

Charlie Kennedy gapes from the back. Lennon is on a mobile phone. The security man is coming down the steps, one step at a time, very slowly. He does not look happy. He has clipped the radio to his belt, and in the silence everyone can hear a small sibilant voice saying, 'Mick, come in, over, Mick are you there, come in, over.' The security man ignores the voice. He has already stretched one hand in front of him, fingers open, as though anticipating the final lunge. Professor Dawkins is two steps behind him. When they reach the last few steps, they push Vanessa to one side very gently.

The security man says, 'Excuse me, miss.' The radio crackles again.

'What is he doing now?' the voice says. 'Mick, for fuck's sake gimme something.' The security man looks at Tom.

Tom takes a deep breath. *Now is the time*, he thinks. *Now or never*.

'I *know!*' he shouts. 'I'm going to tell you the truth.'

Vanessa will understand, he thinks. *And some of the better ones. It will not be wasted on them.*

'Take it easy there, sir,' the security man says.

They see him bend down and fiddle with something behind the podium. The security man thinks, *Sweet Jesus, not a gun*. He feels paralysed, unbearably exposed. He hears what sounds like the clunk of a plug inserted in a socket, or a magazine fitting into place.

When Tom straightens again, he has a piece of electric flex in his hand, the end pared away, a forked tongue of copper at the end of it.

'Jesus,' the security man says. 'Cut the power.' He unclips the radio from his waist and hisses into it, 'Cut the power in here, for Christ's sake.'

The radio voice crackles back, 'Repeat the last message, Mick, over.'

'This is the message,' Tom says quietly. He holds the flex in front of his face; the serpent tongue flashes dull copper at him. 'I still have tenure here,' he says.

He opens his mouth and bites down hard on the wires.

Surrender

Thus we went down, circle by circle, things closing in as we went. 'Go to the Molo Bevorello,' he said. 'Pay at the little kiosk. There will be a ferry waiting. Do not fall asleep on the seat, in the shade, or you will visit each island in turn and come back to the same place. When you wake you will have passed through the past, the present and future and you will have to begin again.'

Or perhaps he did not say so much.

Now I see him standing on the quay with the fishing co-op as backdrop. Men are taking boxes out of cars and passing them into the darkness. A *paranza* with its weighted net is unloading. The little buses and cars wait for us to disembark. When we step ashore we will enter another world. I feel the shiver of the crossing, the shifting paradigms. Everything will be the same and different on this shore. When we turn to look back at the ship, we will be looking outwards: though the same crossing will be there, we will notice something uncertain in the light, or a ripple in the air. A turn in the tide of the fluid we breathe. The world is always novel from an island.

Noisily, amid the cacophony of homecomings and departures, Jim embraces Terry, then me, and leads us to the golf cart that is the island taxi, the only thing small enough to negotiate the narrow streets and lanes. How often has he told this one detail in his letters that are themselves like poems? The *vicoli* of the island so narrow there are no real taxis. They drive like crazy. And I have rehearsed the discovery so frequently that when I see them they are unreal. From the back seat we smile like pilgrims at everything while the driver swings between crooked houses, in and out of the sun, and there are times that if we placed our elbows on the armrest, some wall would clip them off. Lemons glow like weak bulbs, small intense oranges reach for the hand. Garish pelargonium, bougainvillea, hibiscus, gardenia. Every once in a while, the sea winking like broken glass.

At the hotel the owner and his wife greet us. They are gracious, welcoming. We are led upstairs to the rooms, which are bare, clean and full of light from the big ill-fitting windows. A tiny balcony looks out on the middle branches of an ancient bougainvillea. On the corridor between Terry's room and mine, we embrace in solemn silence. A brief symmetry.

Jim has his work. Or so he tells us. He lives in a room in a different hotel. It has become his by-occupation: he calls himself the colonial power. The room faces down across a courtyard of uneven slabs and down a corridor that becomes a side entrance to the hotel. He has everything he needs. A shabby, arthritic laptop that groans and whistles when he saves something onto a disk, that drops dead without warning when the battery runs low, the screen faded so much that it is difficult to read what he writes; a line of books separated from the line above it by a plank, the bottom row holding up the top, the whole topped by a weighty Cambridge Italian Dictionary; a small camping cooker on which he heats coffee and other things. A variety of bottles of wine. Only two glasses. He asks us to steal one from our hotel. 'They'll give you glasses in the bathroom. They'll never miss one. Say you broke it.'

Terry says it sounds just like the shabby flats we used to have when we were in college. Broken beds and chairs whose joints had come unglued and mice. We all remember the beds.

He has lived there for three years. He's clean, apart from a little weed. The book is coming along nicely. He earns a crust by teaching English. And, of course, bowing to Terry, there is the generous advance. The room is cheap because he occupies it all year round, though it can be cold in the winter. Dawkins sends him things. Reviewing brings windfalls.

'Did you do your reading?' he wants to know on the first evening. 'Did you do your homework?'

'Yes.'

'*Nel mezzo del cammin di nostra vita,* he recites aloud, *mi ritrovai per una selva oscura, che la diritta via era smarrita.*'

People turn to look at him. A smartly dressed woman smiles. He continues into the second verse, standing up, the scraping of the chair imposing a partial silence into which the beautiful ordinary *terza rima* falls like the ingratiating words of a seducer. The waiters purse their lips and raise their eyebrows at each other. He ends at 'So bitter it is that scarcely death is worse, but I will speak of the good I found there and also certain other things I learned.' There is polite clapping at the other tables, and he bows and smiles, bows and smiles. Terry pulls him back into his chair. She glares in mock exasperation.

He sits and the smile fades quickly. 'They all learn Dante at school, excerpts in every textbook, the way we had Shakespeare,' he says. 'They all know that part.' He stares at the heaped rings of squid on his plate. 'The middle of the walk of life,' he says. 'The heart of life. It's the first line. Perhaps *because* it's the first. Seven hundred years have turned it into a cliché. I don't know what to do with it. The middle of the footpath of our life? The crown of life's road? Halfway in the stroll of existence? The shortcut to death? The inside track.' He laughs bitterly. 'It's such a banal opening.'

'How far did you get?' Terry asks. He hears the professional undertone.

'The book will be ready in a month. I'm at the tidying-up stage.'

Neither of us believes it. He stares defiantly.

Terry says, 'I think you said that last year in your October letter. I think I have a copy in my bag in my room.'

Around the tine of his fork he hangs a piece of squid so white it is almost artificial. He holds it up for a moment, then puts it in his mouth.

'My printer is shagged at present. I'm waiting for a new one to arrive. It was supposed to be here today. Tomorrow at the latest. I'll run it off for you then.'

'That would be great,' Terry says. The tone is acid. 'They said to me before I left: "Get him to show you what he's done, otherwise he'll lie about it." So . . .' Something leaves a bad taste in our mouths. Not the squid.

Terry pays for the meal in the Bar Dal Cavaliere, carefully folding the receipt into a section of her wallet, and this simple transaction gives her the right to insult him, to challenge his credibility. The night is thick with electricity.

'And you, Charlie,' he says. 'What do you have?'

I tell them about my job. I tell them about the in-fighting and the campus politics, the small triumphs of academic life. My last paper. A projected study of Irish political poetry. The students I can boast of. I do not tell them about the careful pattern that has become the geography of my days: the streets I do not walk, the bars I do not visit. About how nobody calls unexpectedly, because an unexpected knock on the door could mean death. About the meta-language in which the name of a street or a school or a friend establishes an entire history, a tribe, a politics, a future. There are no innocent words where I live. The weight of meaning is unbearable, and so the decent thing to do is to mean as little as possible. I do not mention that I heard the

Omagh bomb explode as I went to visit a colleague that Saturday morning. That I had the window of the car open. That I knew it had to be a bomb. But, I notice, my hands shake as I talk.

As we walk home, boys race Vespas down the hill at terrifying speed. They bump and twist over the uneven basalt slabs that make the road surface. Couples stroll towards us. A family group. Three grandparents, two sets of parents, two children. One child runs into the shadow between the lamps calling insistently that the other is afraid. 'Hai paura. Hai paura.' I recognise the words. Grandfather remonstrates: 'Be quiet,' he says, 'people are asleep.'

And the sound of someone tidying cutlery comes down from one of the high blank walls where the houses turn their backs on the passer-by.

'I don't ever wish I was married,' he says, 'but I surely wish I had kids.'

'How's your Italian?' he says to me, and I tell him that it's coming back slowly since I came. I stopped doing the courses a long time ago. I got lazy.

The hotel is asleep. The night duty is thrown across three seats in the lobby, the television flickering at him, its blank back towards us. We take our keys from the desk and tiptoe to the stairs. He calls a sleepy buonanotte. The marble wall is cool to the touch. In my room the window has been left open. There is lightning along the coast towards Cumæ – the sibyl crackling about doom, thunder in rapid salvoes. Delicate lightning in the blue gloom. The great black peak of Ischia, at its base a thousand lights. I can make out traffic signals, cars moving down a hill. There is no breeze even up here so high above the beach and the streets. The lightning flickers and dances and the drums roll like marchers warming up for the advance. Far away in Ireland, a mile, two miles from my office, they would be standing in circles beating out the rantan, the huge hollow bellies that farted anger and spite. Warming up for weeks for the Glorious Twelfth. Tradition. There were other traditions too – like beating Jews, like raping Moslems – that were founded on hatred: nobody was queuing up to give them parity of esteem.

She rises, sleepy and heavy with the heat, at half past eleven and suggests we spend the afternoon at the beach. Jim is to get on with installing his new printer and running off the first draft of whatever he has finished while we spend a few hours sunning and swimming, relaxing and talking over old times.

It is, I recognise, part of her strategy. 'Come with me, Charlie,' her phone call said. 'It'll be a bit of a holiday.' And I thought it would mean a few days, a week, alone with her after all this time. And she may have been thinking the same.

But most of all she knew I was the only one he trusted. He would never trust her. Now she will take me down to the sea, to soften me up, to keep me on side. And when we get back to the hotel, the first draft as far as Canto XXVI will be waiting for us. Then we can begin in earnest. 'He must do it, Charlie,' she said. 'I'm afraid he'll self-destruct any minute now. I've spent years on this.'

Terry sitting in her office, making calls, dictating letters, *she* has spent years on this.

We each hire a chair and an umbrella, the first we find. The matronly ladies who bring their children down slightly later all move further along. The lilting sound of the unknown lulls us, and we sleep with our feet towards the ancient sea, our heads towards the crumbling pumice cliffs, until I am awakened by a dream in which I can smell rotten vegetables.

The smell is still there. A breeze has developed, and small waves are pushing an object toward me that I had originally assumed to be a small rock forty feet offshore but which is now, clearly, a dead turtle. The shell is there, forming a bowl in which the meat putrefies. The underside, some kind of softer armour, is broken. There is no head, no flippers. When it surges on a wave, it provokes a tiny storm of dark sand, clouding the water. The sun has come round to shine in our faces under the brim of the umbrella, and the soles of my feet feel hot.

The women are departing, gathering bags and children. All along the beach, the chairs that had been filling when I fell asleep are emptying now, their angles pointed back towards the village. Where has the day gone? A man in pale blue overalls comes down and strips in a single elegant procedure to a fragment of cloth that I take to be his bathing trunks. He walks forward purposefully and then launches himself at the water. A boy comes down the steps behind and begins to clap the chairs closed. Seeing Terry asleep in the shade, he begins to close them silently. He unties the strings of the umbrellas and they fold down suddenly. He smiles at me.

I wake Terry. I see her tumble out of some happy place. She sniffs the air and makes a face. 'It's the dead turtle,' I say. I point.

She stands up abruptly. 'Jesus Christ! Why didn't you wake me? For fuck's sake.'

It is no use to protest that I am just awake myself. She gathers her things and stuffs them into a net bag. She pulls a cardigan on. She walks past the careful boy and up the steps. I give him a thousand lire note and say '*Ciao*' tentatively. He says '*Ciao*' back.

I try to keep up. I watch her sandals – the way when she tilts forward onto the ball of her foot, the strap at the heel slips down and a gap develops briefly. The way the tendon at the back of her calf becomes a smooth curve of muscle, a bent bow. Two tendons work the hinge of her knee. I have been falling behind for ten years now, publishing less, relying on older and older notes, old friends, the same places. A failing college professor. A forgettable teacher. Whereas all impediments have failed to slow her down or have been discarded. She is the commissioning editor now, the peak of her profession, a successful woman with a string of major publications. She talks about her list. The things that are on her list and the things she would like to have on it. Jim's translation, for instance. Every now and then she flaps the edges of the cardigan she has thrown over her bikini. 'Jesus Christ,' she says, 'I think that smell is still in it.'

The window of Jim's room is open, and we can see a brown cardboard package on top of the stack of books at the far end – the printer still in its case. In the outdoor dining area on the right of the passage, Jim is talking to a very old man, and there is a bottle of wine on the table. The rattan roof throws a slatted shade on them. A lizard scuttles for cover as we pass. His tail is twice as long as his body. Jim waves us over with an empty glass, but Terry carries on. 'I'll see you at our hotel,' she says, moving on quickly, and unspoken is the implication that he is my responsibility. That she has delegated him to me.

'That man,' he tells me excitedly, 'is a genius. Do you believe that, Charlie? He tells me stories, amazing stories . . .'

'You can't keep this up, Jim,' I say. I have been told to say it. I know I am letting him down. 'Terry is pissed off. She told me to tell you she doesn't believe in this project. They may ask for the advance back.'

'Fuck that. They never ask for their money back and you

know it. What are they going to do? Sue my computer off me? They can have it. I'll still have a pen. They won't be able to stop me. And if they do, the contract's off. I'll be able to hawk the book around. Penguin would be interested, maybe Faber. It's going to be sensational. Fuck *Beowulf* man! This is about God and love not some fucking giant alligator.'

'They won't pay the next advance.'

Dignity then. 'I never expected it. The contract says *on delivery of manuscript*.'

'But you wrote asking for it.'

He explodes. 'For my fucking printer! Not for me.'

'Terry says give it to her on disk and she can read it on her laptop.'

Silence.

'Jim.'

'That'd be the same as giving her the manuscript.'

'Exactly.'

Very quiet. Looking at me. 'No.'

In the humidity our clothes are sticky. It is like being covered in a fine layer of sweat. Her blouse is loose at the waist, and every now and then she lifts it and flaps some air in. We sit on the terrace under a bougainvillea in full purple flower and watch the lizards waiting for flies behind the lights. She is drinking a limoncello and I am drinking water. I have decided I need to be careful. She is tipsy and sentimental, talking about old times. I notice that her language has coarsened in melancholy. Fuck this and fuck that. Or perhaps it is the drink. She keeps her knees spread but closes them with a snap sometimes to circulate the air. We laugh over distant escapades, close shaves, stale jokes. There is nothing like old times to soften the hard rim of the here and now.

'Charlie, will you help me?'

Her face is close to mine. I can smell the wine and the sweet limoncello.

'You saw the sample pieces he sent. It's going to be something, you know that. He trusts you, he always did. I'm an editor not a friend, I know that. But I do so want this book to come out. For him. It'll make his name. But he must finish it. The time is right. Will you help me? You're his friend.'

'That's what you brought me for,' I say. 'I'm at your disposal.'

'But do you believe in this book? Do you have faith in him?'

'There's too much faith in the world, Terry. But what you showed me – I know what I saw. It's his best work yet.'

I watch as she fiddles with the thin glass. And flaps air under her shirt. What I have said is not enough.

'How can you stick it, Charlie?' she says. 'Up there. Aren't you ever afraid?'

'Are you?' I say.

'Don't give me that London-is-as-dangerous-as-Belfast crap, Charlie.'

'How long is it since you took the underground at night?'

'That's true for every city.'

'I like the place,' I said. 'And a lot of the people. They're interesting. They're direct. Honest.'

'Fuck honest. You mean they don't say enough to tell lies.'

'Which of us does?'

Later I said, 'You may not be able to understand this, Terry. I kind of feel I've gone this far, and I'd like to see how it pans out. There's a ceasefire now, you know. Peace talks. Everything is different.' By which I mean they use baseball bats instead of guns, tyre irons instead of bombs.

Jim tells me that I was once a completely crass person. The implication, I think, is that I haven't changed much, that the word completely might no longer be necessary. He now refuses to let me into his room on the grounds that I am of the other camp. I knock and he responds by calling me False Sinon. 'You brought the horse in,' he calls, 'and then you opened the gates. Torture yourself that all the world knows it.' And then I hear him laughing.

Like with most things he says, I sense a passage behind that I cannot at once locate. It gives his speech a bizarre, slightly hollow, echoing quality.

He keeps me waiting at his door, and I am suspicious of the sweet smell that comes through the cracks. When he comes out, he is unnaturally cheerful. 'You recognised the allusion?' he asks. 'Sinon was the guy who opened the gates of Troy. He's way down in hell, according to my man Dante. No offence, Charlie. No offence, man.'

I try to see his eyes, but he looks away.

'Let's go for a swim,' he says.

'The beach is called Ciracello,' he tells me. 'Famous for being the only beach on the island that has never been famous for anything.'

On the way down the hill he is preoccupied. He hums and talks to himself. Sometimes he beats out a rhythm in his palm. He greets a leathery old man outside the vegetable shop with '*Salve Tommaso, eh?*' And the old man replies with '*Salve, Jim.*' How long has he been living here? And how can he survive?

'I'll never do the *Paradiso* or the *Purgatorio*,' he says suddenly. 'They just don't interest me. Hell is where it's all at. Next I want to write a play about Paolo and Francesca. And that bastard Malatesta. It has all the ingredients. When she says, you know, *nessun maggior dolore che ricordarsi del tempo felice nella miseria*, I truly believe it. There is no greater pain than to recall a happier time in a time of grief. That'll be the last line of the play. Curtain. It'll be about love and memory. That's my next project after I get the monkey off my back.'

The monkey is the translation. Terry says it is not uncommon for authors involved in long projects to feel resentful, even though the project is paying their wages. They have already mastered most of the difficulties and are anxious to move on to the next challenge. 'It's human,' she says. I detect a note of disbelief, as though she does not believe in the humanity of writers.

The beach is crowded because it is Saturday. Close to the steps, there are the chairs that Terry and I hired on our second day. Young women with impossible bodies lounge on them, trying to avoid the shade of the umbrellas. Some are topless and their breasts have paler triangles, the nipples set off-centre. Jim stands and surveys the throng. 'Conveyor belt beauty,' he says. 'When you come to Italy first, you can't take your eyes off them. The beautiful women with the perfect hips and perfect legs and asses. You think the gods have indeed smiled on them. After a while you start to wish for some individuality, for someone with a little more flesh or small breasts. Notice the number of bottle blondes? *La bella figura*. They're obsessed with surfaces. It's a plague of clones. The Italian for girlfriend is *bimbo*, or was anyway.'

He swims very far out. A line of orange buoys marks the limit that boats are permitted to approach the beach. He swims out there, so far that against the sun I can hardly see his head. I follow him by the occasional splash. The beach underfoot is too hot. I spread my towel as far as possible and sit hunched to avoid touching the burning sand. Where the water washes in, it is black. The peak of Ischia is in the distance, suggesting the immanence of holocaust, the dormant Epomeo trailing a wisp of cloud as though it smokes. At our backs, somewhere behind the hill, twenty miles away, are Vesuvius and the fields of fire in which a man is petrified where he falls down and a dog dies at his post watching the black ash and the smoke. It was no surrender there, too, and duty and the fearless few. Pliny taking his notes, the whole thing too good to be missed for a historian. I have known a few of those.

I am aware of the whiteness of my skin against the black sand, the brown and black bodies. The flab at my waist. It feels sinful, not in the way of great sinners, but truly sordid and unpleasant. I should take care of myself. This woman that is between the two of us, driving him, frightening me: so beautiful still, so desirable. Nothing has been resolved in all those years. I fell in love with her at twenty-five.

I am beginning to resent my intermediary status and our morning and evening tactical conferences. Is he writing? Has he shown me any of the text? What does he say about it? Has he discussed the technicalities? There is something more here than I can fathom. As before, I am out of my depth.

'He tells me nothing,' I say. 'We talk about women, the way men do.' This exasperates her. 'We went swimming, and he told me he intended to write a play about Paolo and Francesca. He quoted a line about there being no greater pain than to remember a happy time in a sad time. He went too far out, beyond the safe marks. I worried.'

She rejoins sharply. 'A time of misery. I know. That was in the sample section he sent us. It's Canto V.' She seems disturbed. 'Why does he keep going back to the same things,' she says. 'Why can't he move on? I so want him to finish this. It'll make his name. Make his reputation. We all know he deserves more than he's got. This'll put him centre stage again. It'll be his

Beowulf.' I have noticed that she thinks like this: the new *Bonfire of the Vanities,* the new *Longitude.* When she talks about the books she is working on, she is always enthusiastic – it's always *the new* something else. As though each thing that is valuable belongs to a template stamped out by someone more original.

And I want to say that Dante is not sexy, with his big hooked nose and his flap cap and his talk about angels and punishment and his desire for revenge on the people who sent him into exile from his beloved Florence. *Monsters and dragons are in, God is out,* I think. This will be a fine translation, but it won't have him giving readings in a football stadium. And I am worried about his state of mind and whether he is looking after his health. 'There's ants in my computer,' he told me yesterday. 'They come out of slots in the casing. At first I thought I'd evict them, but nothing shifts the bastards. I'm thinking maybe they'll figure something out. You know the way ants have this kind of collective mind. Maybe they'll get at the mother board. Or figure out a way to make themselves heavy enough to press the keys. What if I start to get messages? Jesus, I couldn't take it if the fuckers started to write about me.'

I never know when he is serious now. Never know when he is taking the piss. I am lost.

'Why did he do this to himself?' Terry says.

She drinks too much. Two *aperitivo*s before dinner. A full bottle every night at our table. Afterwards, a night cap or two. Grappa for her, a kind of Italian poitín, and sometimes limoncello. When she drinks, she asks searching questions. 'Why haven't you found a woman, Charlie?' Why hasn't she found a man? Not men, but a man. 'I don't want to be a serial shagger,' she says. 'I want to settle down. It's almost too late for kids. What happened to us all? How do people work in this climate?' Between twelve and four she sleeps. 'When I'm at home I never sleep during the day,' she says. 'Why am I sleeping so much?' Then Jim comes out of the shadows. He is wearing plastic sandals, a dark T-shirt, grubby grey trousers. He is a little out of breath climbing the short slope up to the terrace. For the first time, I notice the strange pallor under his tan, the rings around his eyes, the way his hair seems to sit lifelessly on his head like some kind of rough cloth. 'We are going to a concert,' he says. 'Come on, no slacking.'

The island band is playing for St John's night in the little village of Corricella. The streets are full of strollers, couples arm in arm, families, single men and women. This evening walk is the quintessential Italian thing for me, the mothers and daughters arm-in-arm, the boys on Vespas or in small cars, revving the engines and waving. It is a familial chaos, the crazy art of community. They call to each other or to people in windows or on stairways. This is a different life. 'I want to stay here,' I tell him. 'Find me a job teaching English and I'll stay for ever.'

'No, you don't want to stay here,' he says. 'You're a kind of Narcissus, falling in love with your own mirror image. You're better off up there in Belfast with those hard-arsed Free Presbyterians in that godforsaken place you're teaching. This is the kind of life you would *like* to want, Charlie. But it would be a different you that wanted it.'

'Fuck you and your bullshit,' I say, surprising myself. Since moving to Northern Ireland my expletives have weakened and fallen silent. 'Blast,' I say. Or 'Damn.' Sometimes even, 'Goodness.' The old words feel wet and hard in my mouth. 'What do you know about Belfast? No more than you see on TV. What do you know about the people there? You haven't a clue.'

'No,' he says, not in the least affected by my outburst, 'you belong up there all right. Up in the hard North where a bargain is a bargain and nothing over. You'd be ripe and rotten here in a month.'

Steps lead down a sheer cliff, and the crescent-shaped village is below us, sheltered from the open sea by a concrete reef. The pastel-coloured houses are joined at the top or bottom or by fantastic staircases, or shared doorways, stepped up three or four or five floors with their back against the cliff. Some of the rooms must be cut into rock. The buildings are crazy, but the boats are neat and orderly, and the nets lie in piles along the quay. The music has started, and the sound of a *cor anglais* rises to meet us. We stand at the top and watch Terry stepping neatly down into the darkness. Her light skirt swirls as she drops. There's a change in the air, a breeze ruffling the darkness out by the breakwater. The boats are sawing on their moorings. It has come suddenly, whatever it is: sudden and unprovided for.

'It's too late, Charlie,' he says. 'It takes years before you're any good at living in a place like this. I'm only starting now. And it's probably too late.'

He's right. And Terry, too. Where I live, it is better to say as little as possible. Careful sentences, practised and positive, modulated. We live with the fear of other people's faith. A false word could cost a life or a leg. People have been killed in error. *In error.* Afterwards, nobody apologises. My next-door neighbour lost three fingers of his left hand when a sheet of plate glass took them off. He had been evacuated from the travel agent's office where he worked, but the bomb exploded prematurely. He never talks about it. We pass the time of day, but he doesn't wave. It helps to be polite. Better again, say nothing. I am tending in that direction. A day will come when I will walk to the pub for my evening pint and walk home again without uttering a word. The silence is a tangible thing. People take sustenance from it and wear away in the process: in the consanguinity of bloodbaths. I take a deep breath and push out against the silence.

'She means what she says, Jim. She's not doing this for herself. I mean, there's no money in poetry. You know that. She's had to fight off the marketing people and the money men to keep you on the list. She believes in you. She believes this is going to be an important work.'

The band strikes up 'Colonel Bogey' and suddenly there is a spring to his step. 'Come on, man,' he says. 'We'll miss the best of it.'

You're working for her, Charlie, you know that. I know it too. I forgive you. It's the following night and we're watching the activity in the port. A ferry is coming in at high speed because of the crosswind. Suddenly it sweeps up a tight circle and drops its anchor. Then the water is boiling forward from its stern. Bright lights shine down onto the afterdeck where a handful of passengers watches us. A man appears on the quay and waits for the rope to be thrown. Late into the night, the ferries move between the islands on a bottomless sea: by day they are purposeful white shapes among the pleasure craft.

'I'm not working for anybody,' I say. I am aware of a momentary equilibrium: the slightest motion and I fall. 'I'm just lost. I agreed to come because I thought I could persuade you to finish the translation. I'm not making a secret of that. She rang me up and asked me. "You're his friend," she said. "He'll trust you."' I look steadily at him. I want him to understand. 'First of all, I believe she's right. Secondly, it's important for you. When Terry sent me the draft copy, I knew exactly why she was so anxious to get you to wrap it up. It'll make her name and it'll remake yours. It's as simple as that.'

He laughs and shakes his head.

'It's true,' I say.

'You talk a lot of bullshit even for a college teacher. You always were full of it.'

'You have to come home.'

'Fuck that. I am at home.'

'Look – Jim, please.'

All day a *sirocco* has been blowing over the back of the island; a thin, high layer of cloud; the sun a pale orange light behind clouded glass. It was difficult to decide where the horizon began and ended. The sea on the south eastern side was rough and waves broke white: but where we sit now, in the lee of the port captain's hut, it is pleasant enough, although a fine dust settles on every surface. 'Forget it, Charlie,' he says. Then suddenly: 'Are you fucking her?' I shake my head and stare at him. 'Are you sure?'

'Look, Jim, if I was, I'd know, all right.'

He pats me on the back. 'Poor Charlie Kennedy. She's not for you. See what she has become. It would be like fucking a rope or . . . anything functional. She's a machine. She has no feelings. She's a unit in the system.'

I tell him once again that he doesn't know what he's talking about. That she's my friend, too. And he apologises. 'You know,' he says, 'I'd like to love her. In a way I do. I'd like to want her, but I don't. I don't really want anything or anybody. It's not her, it's me.'

He has reached the end of some kind of tether, I see. The skin is looser around his eyes and taut over his cheeks. He seems even thinner than when we saw him first ten days ago. I have the strange impression that a metamorphosis has taken place in him between strength and weakness, the first becoming the second in the reaction. And I know, too, that he is lying: that after all these years he still remembers her body the way a bird remembers the summer.

'Look at these guys.' He nods at the people spilling out of the ferry and into the tiny orange bus that will take them home. 'They work on the mainland, but they live here. They think they have the best of both worlds, but they're as thin and as flat as paper. One touch and they tear. Either you live on the mainland or you live on the island. You can't belong to both. Did I ever tell you my father ran out on us? When I was ten.'

'It's in your bio. Half the world knows it.'

He gives me a suspicious look, then grins.

'Tomorrow I'm going to show you something. I want you to see it before you go back.'

When I get back to the hotel, the wind is shaking the lemon groves, the gloomy bougainvillea. There are brighter windfalls in the dust. A curious musical whistling noise pervades the hotel. 'La casa delle fantasmagorie,' Vincenzo, the night duty, says, imitating the sound. He points to the ceiling. 'Il vento.' He is apologetic.

I knock on her door, but there is no answer. I hear only the hotel's eerie whistling. I want to tell her that I think there is something seriously wrong, that I think he's losing it, that maybe we've pushed him too far. I am prepared to believe in her sleep. That she lies on her bed in something light and cool, dreaming her dreams, with one hand under her cheek, or lying along the pillow. I tiptoe along the corridor of the house of the phantoms.

But sometime after midnight the silence wakes me. The wind is gone and the room is stifling. I open the shutters and step out onto the balcony. The bougainvillea looks enormous in the darkness. There is no moon. For no reason I can explain, I am aware that Terry is watching me from her balcony. I turn and look at her. She is there for a moment, then she is gone. I go back to bed. Then I hear her tapping at my door.

She shakes in my hands. 'Be nice to me,' she says. 'I can't stand it.'

As I fuck her, I think of the Trojan horse. But it is not like fucking a piece of wood or a rope. There are things he does not understand. And afterwards we console each other with silence, by our even breathing, a kind of peace. A film of moisture separates us where our foreheads almost touch.

In the morning we drink from the only remaining glass. She sits with her back against the wall, the sheet rucked across her lap. I hold one breast and circle my thumb around the nipple. She looks down and smiles. 'Come to London with me,' she says. 'You'll find a job. Get out of that dead end you're in. Go someplace that has a future.' And I agree, not wanting to lose this moment.

'This is Pozzo Vecchio,' he says. 'This is the most beautiful place.'

A tiny circular-domed church at the same level as the road, then rank after rank of stairs, the walls lined with marble graves that swirl downwards circle after circle. The stairs relate to each other in complex ways, intersecting, parting, blending, twisting, paralleling – like an Escher print. Down on the flat at the bottom of the last set of steps, almost at the same level as the sea, is a conventional graveyard with the usual mix of ordinary and extraordinary headstones – flat marble slab or angel with trumpet, simple crosses, bas-relief of the resurrection, Calvary, or the Virgin Mary. Beyond the wall, people play in the sand. There are children's voices, the sound of a football and brave goalkeeping and spectacular passing. He stops there with his back to the sea. 'Look,' he says.

The strange geometry rises steadily towards the little church, the graves mounting or descending according to point of view, and at the top, leaning curiously on the wall and looking down on us, a man in blue overalls.

He begins to recite.

> *Above those gates I saw a thousand shadows*
> > *Haled from Heaven, who bellowed at us:*
> > *What are you who, without passing,*
> *Travel in the kingdom of the dead?*

The man in blue overalls is straining to hear. The simple lines echo among the marble slabs.

Jim pauses for effect, or perhaps to listen for echoes.

'The funny thing about translating,' he says, 'is that the closer you get, the more you realise that the gap between you and the work is unbridgeable. It's this tiny space where everything is so intense, so concentrated, that if you stepped into it the forces would tear you apart. The space between two languages is too small to be crossed.'

The man in the blue overalls is smoking, and a translucent cloud surrounds him like a glory.

'I've made arrangements to be buried here,' he says after a time. 'With the priest. He doesn't know anything about me except that I come from Ireland. Ireland is a very devout place, as far as he's concerned, famous for its resistance to heresy. He doesn't know about your crowd up north, Charlie.'

Terry chuckles. 'It's going to be a long funeral. I hope you don't expect us to carry your fucking coffin from Ireland to here.'

Her words shock him. I see him shiver. He begins to recite the same lines in Italian, louder this time, as though to reach the workman overhead. '*Chi è costui, che senza morte va per il regno della morta gente . . .*'

'Come off it, Jim,' she says. 'You're giving me the creeps. Finish the fucking book and stop messing me around.'

'I have finished it.'

'You have in your ass.'

He chuckles. 'It's a long time since I heard that particular colloquialism.'

There is a real smile tugging at the corners of her lips – the first one I've seen since we came. Once I thought they were made for each other. What happened to them?

She begins to lecture him. 'You need to get back home,' she says. 'You need to get a fellowship somewhere or a residency. Better again, start lecturing. Jesus, you could lecture on the influence of Dante on someone. Anyone. *The Waste Land.* They'd fall over themselves to get you. Try the States. You need to get a grip on yourself. Finish the book. Once it comes out, they'll all want you . . .'

Gently he repeats, 'I *have* finished the book.'

She steps in front of him, her face flushed with anger. 'For fuck's sake, stop! Stop lying! Do you know how much I have riding on you? My fucking reputation, that's what.'

He takes a computer disk from his trousers pocket and hands it to her. I see that it is neatly labelled *The Inferno – Dante Alighieri, Trans. James Henchion.* She takes it from his hand and turns it over as though the underside will reveal a rotten substructure. She stares. Then she looks at me and I shake my head, a tiny stiff movement meaning *He never told me, I knew nothing.* Maybe I detect a tear in her eye, maybe not. 'Jim,' she says softly, 'you didn't rush it? Did you?'

'As a matter of fact, I finished it months ago. I just couldn't let go. How many years am I at it now?'

They laugh together, easily, warmly. She takes his hand.

'Thank you.'

'No, thank *you*. You drove me this far. I'd never have kept going but for you. I wouldn't have done it for anybody else.'

'Is there anything special you want . . . ? An epigraph or anything?'

'Yes. I want the words I just quoted, in both Italian and my English, under my name. I'll write to you about it. I have cancer. A bad one. I'm not going home. When you pay me the rest of my advance, I'm renting a small house just up there. So I'm in the parish. I may even start going to mass in that church. The *padre* is going to be pleased.'

At four in the morning, the island is buried in fog. Prospero is at work. And even in sleep the isle is noisy. At the first wink of light, the sparrows start to hope. A cock crows somewhere. An engine turns over down the hill in the port. 'Fog in the morning is a sign of a good day,' my father used to say. But here it is never anything else, so no signs are necessary. I move her hand and she shifts a little and murmurs something incomprehensible. I cannot resist the thought that I am the one she came to after all these years. Although I don't know why, and the possibilities are worrying. And now I know I am going to lose her, the stubborn Northern cold surfacing in me at last, the no surrender. I try to think how I will tell her, and I wonder, too, if it will matter to her now that she has her book. I open the French windows and sit on the tiny balcony and look out towards Ischia and wait for things to lift. My heart is a sparrow. I try to work things out, but I cannot escape the feeling that there is something shameful about all of us. We are going home because we have what we want. What we came for. And he is afraid. The fog is beginning to burn away. Already the spine of Vivara is visible. Houses are morphing out of the grey. The colours remind me of home. Two pink houses, a gold house, a yellow house, a grey.

The Meanings of Wind

Sitting in the drowning car, Paddy thinks of Thucydides. A change of wind during a naval engagement throws the Spartan ships into disarray but gives the Athenians the opportunity to attack. The wind was real, according to Thucydides, and both sides reported it faithfully, but the same wind has a different meaning for each side. The Athenian commander saw it as the dawn wind, a regular occurrence, and he made it part of his plan of attack, waiting for it to rise, knowing it would disadvantage the enemy. On the other hand, the wind is seen by the Spartans as an unlucky accident that favoured the other side, a malign chance, because the Spartans were not equipped to understand the disaster that had befallen them.

They had both seen the dawn wind rise that morning. He got up to draw the curtains, and at the same time she stretched and propped her pillow up against the bedhead. 'What time is it, Paddy? Christ, I thought it was time to go.'

Just at that moment, out on the street outside their window, the big flat leaves on the poplars began to move.

'It's the dawn wind,' he said.

They watched it progress along the trees, each leaf moving singly, on its own individual and ultimately chaotic current, but together forming an impression of a vast restless crowd.

They made love, as they often did early in the morning. 'You're always harder,' she liked to tell him. She ran her hands up and down his sides and came just before he did. She smiled and said, 'Practice makes perfect.' He liked her sounds, especially when he tortured her a little by continuing to move after she came. 'Oh, oh,' she would say. 'Oh God.'

She slept for a time. He lay on his side staring at the wind and listening to the sound of the early-morning traffic. An ambulance went by blaring: Santa Maria Nuova was just around the corner. Then they got up and went to breakfast.

Later in the day, the wind would trouble him. By then it had turned into a full breeze that shook everything and bent the cypresses double along the motorway. Signs warning of crosswinds had to be taken seriously. Clouds scudded across an enamel sky and below, on his left, the neat olive groves moved uncertainly. *Everyone is uneasy about wind,* he thought. *It has no assurance in it. From day to day, place to place, winds are fickle.*

He turned on to a side road and headed up into the hills. The road narrowed and twisted, and every now and then went through a ravine. Signs predicted the collapse of the surrounding cliffs and bluffs. On his left, the road was lined with a special spring-mounted fence that was designed to absorb the force of falling rock and neutralise it. Every mile or so, there was a gallery of concrete where rockfalls were common. He stopped at a wayside van and bought a slice of spicy pork in a chunk of bread. The owner read a comic and a radio played in the background. 'Two days ago there was an earthquake,' the owner said. 'A small one. A tremor. The direct road to Norcia is closed. You must go by Castelluccio.'

He cursed. This was a thirty-mile detour.

Thunderheads were gathering over the Sibylline Mountains. There would be rain before long.

Up he goes, higher and deeper. The mountains crowd down on him with their capstone of cloud. He comes out on the high karstic plain in thunder and lightning and sees the ruined hill village of Castelluccio ahead of him. There's a restaurant there, he knows. His mobile phone is registering no signal. People come here in camper vans and tour coaches so they can say they've been in the most remote village in Italy. A paradox. For a moment he thinks of stopping for lunch, and to make a phone call, but instead he drives straight through even though his belly is rumbling. Past the village. Along the flat grassland. Rain sweeps off his windscreen, the wipers weighted by it. He turns his headlights on full. Outside, the temperature has dropped ten degrees, but inside the cabin it is still hot and the air is humid. Everything irritates him: the squeak of the accelerator, a scratching sound the wipers make as they reach the end of their stroke, a driver coming towards him in the middle of the road.

He pulls over and tries to call ahead to say he's late and why, but the phone is still silent. Probably the lightning has put the antenna out. His daughter, he knows, will be anxious.

Then over the saddle of the mountain and on to that almost vertical road that winds round and down interminably. Here stones and gravel have been washed out by the rain. He slows to a crawl. A rock the size of a football sits in the middle of the road. A thousand feet below, the tree line is boiling, firs and stone pines twisting as though trying to escape: but up here in the lightning and rain, there is no wind. He feels like he is swimming rather than driving, the way ahead vanishing downwards and to the left at every bend. He imagines he is diving into a turbulent sea, but then the wind would be above him, the waves would be above, whereas he knows that, on this mountain, lower down things are much rougher. Lightning and thunder come almost simultaneously now, a second at most between. The thunder is hard, singular, explosive, not rolling like a drumbeat. He pulls in again and sits there in the submarine heat, watching the coloured sceptres of electricity divide the sky and plunge earthwards. *If I survive*, he thinks, *I will tell my wife and make a new start.* He knows his daughter will forgive him. Something hard hits the back wheel. He turns in time to see a slough of gravel come loose and flood across the road. The water around it is peat brown, like menstrual blood. He thinks that if the storm lasts much longer the mountain will swallow him or push him over the side. *So this is the meaning of the wind,* he thinks. He thinks of Thucydides. That morning she had joked that it was an ill wind that didn't blow someone some good. With her legs spread and the air-conditioning full on and the room slowly cooling after their sex.

'When is Paddy coming?' his daughter is saying. She had taken to calling him Paddy since their last trip home two years ago.

Her mother smiles and points upwards. 'The gods are angry,' she says. 'They are tramping around the mountains. Pray Daddy has had the sense to stay in Florence. One day more won't be too long to wait.' But she is laughing when she says it. She is shelling walnuts over a wooden bowl, and the gesture she makes contains her hand, the nutcracker and several falling splinters of shell. 'Make me some tea, there's a good child.'

Two flies above the table, their movements are demented. The sound of the lighter clicking and the gas popping into flame. Light and heat out of nothingness. The will-o'-the-wisp. The kettle begins to groan. She feels sweat gathering at her hairline. In Florence, she knows, Paddy will have the air-conditioning on. They always put him up at a decent place. There will be a mini-bar with cold beer and mineral water.

'I see spots on the window,' her daughter says. 'Look. Rain.'

Then the rain is drumming on the house. In a few moments, the shallow drains are spilling. It pours in sheets off the roof.

'God,' her daughter says. 'That was quick.'

They both stop to watch in awe. A door bangs somewhere.

'There's a heatwave on the plain,' she says, 'and when that happens we always get thunder in the mountains. It's all to do with fronts and warm air and altitude.'

Across the way, the Serafinas' olive trees are dancing. Her daughter points to them. 'Like old men dancing,' she says. 'Old Serafina will be mad.'

'The roads will be closed again.'

'Does that mean Paddy won't be here for dinner?'

'I hope he has more sense.'

'Can I stand in the rain?'

Her mother laughs. Only a child of the Mediterranean lands could want to stand in the rain. If she had grown up in Ireland, she'd sulk at the very mention of the word. But she puts down her nutcracker and her bowl of walnuts and takes her daughter's hand. They go out together and stand on the terrace until they are soaked through, like people who have fallen overboard from a boat. They laugh like them, too, like people who have almost been lost to the sea but instead have been rescued by a millionaire, like people who cannot believe their luck. Away in the distance they hear the rolling cracks of doom, thousands of feet up in the mountains.

'Is it raining in Florence now?' her daughter shouts.

She shakes her head.

'Is it raining up in Castelluccio?'

'Yes. It's bad in Castelluccio now.'

The William Walls

One should not multiply entities unnecessarily.
William of Ockham

In his *History of the Church of Jesus Christ of Latter-day Saints*, Volume 5, Joseph Smith says that he wrestled with William Wall, the most expert wrestler in Ramus, and threw him. This event occurred on a Monday in 1843. Joseph Smith is sometimes known as the Wrestling Prophet. Nothing further is known about the expert wrestler William Wall. We do not know if he was, or became, a Mormon, or if Joseph Smith mentions throwing him as an example of the prophet overcoming evil by the grace of God, or merely to prove that he was a pretty tough prophet as they go.

A cemetery somewhere in the USA contains fifteen Walls, including two Williams, one born 1803, died 1886. His headstone bears the following rhyme:

> *Although he sleeps his memory doeth*
> *And cheering comforts to his mourners grief*
> *He followed virtue as his truest guide*
> *Lived as a Christian as a Christian died.*

'Doeth' is clearly a transcription error and should rhyme with 'grief', but it is difficult to imagine a word that would rhyme and which might be mistaken for 'doeth'. Another possibility is that the word 'live' is missing. Perhaps the stone is chipped or severely eroded on that side. 'Live' chimes nicely with 'grief' and indicates a subtlety not otherwise in evidence in the piece. However, taking the line in isolation, 'wakes' would have been better. The scansion, as is common in such funerary compositions, is irregular in places. Another, probably earlier, grave in the same cemetery simply gives the surname Wall and is marked with fieldstones. What the given name of this antecedent Wall might have been we do not know.

A website called *The Puritan's Mind* lists various important books including, under the heading 'Paedobaptistic', *The History of Infant Baptism in Two Parts* (London, 1697) by William Wall. John Wesley later reduced the entire apparently prolix opus to a mere twenty-one pages eventually published as *Extract from a Late Writer* in 1751. Wall's book appears to have been controversial in the circles in which it was read and gave rise to *Reflections on Mr. Wall's History of Infant Baptism,* by John Gale, which, in turn, brought forth a response from the redoubtable author in the form of *A Defence of the History of Infant Baptism Against the Reflections of Mr. Gale and Others.* The site records a lively interest in the question of baptising infants and, so, many of the other texts may be presumed to relate to William Wall's seminal work, or to have engendered it. My own particular favourite is *Anabaptism: The True Fountain of Independency, Antinomy, Brownism, Familism, and the most of the other errors which for the time do trouble the church of England, Unsealed; Also, the Questions of Paedobaptism and Dipping Handled from Scripture,* by Robert Baillie.

In the oral histories of Denton County, San Antonio, Texas, there is the following account by possibly the toughest of all the William Walls:

> *When we worked, there was always one man stood on watch all the time so that the Indians couldn't slip up on us and shoot us in the back. I have been in lots of fights with them. There was the McLaren family – nearly all of them*

was killed out. Mr. McLaren had gone off on a trade and left Allen Leese there to stay with his family and Allen and Mrs. McLaren was down under the hill making a garden. They heard a racket up at the house and she thought it might be the hogs into her pot of soap she had made and sent Allen up there to scare 'em off. When he got to the top of the hill, the Indians shot him dead and Mrs. McLaren grabbed her two children and broke to run down through the garden and they shot her. She sent the child for help but help come too late. We gave her a drink of water and she died. Well, we followed them Indians clear into Mexico and killed 'em. I was with the bunch that trailed 'em and I took one of Mrs. McLaren's dresses off of an old squaw. Yes, the squaws were wearing her clothes but we sure took 'em off of them.

William Wall was born in 1792 in Dublin, Ireland. He emigrated to New York City. He was already a fine artist by the time he left Dublin. In New York, he helped found the National Academy of Design. He exhibited his work there and at the Pennsylvania Academy of Fine Arts. He became famous for a series of watercolours of the Hudson River area. John and William Hill published a series of engravings based on the watercolours. He seems to have been to and fro to Ireland between 1835 and his eventual retirement there in 1860. William Archibald Wall, his son, was also a landscape painter.

Sarban was the pseudonym of William Wall. He was born near Rotherham in Yorkshire where his father was a guard on a passenger train. He won a scholarship to Jesus College, Cambridge (where he got the cheapest rooms and felt like an outsider). He learned Arabic in his spare time, influenced by the poetry of Flecker, he said. He obtained a posting in the Consular Service in 1933 and spent the rest of his working life there.

Some time in the 1940s, he showed some short stories to Eleanor Alexander, whom he would later marry, and she liked them, suggested alterations and offered to find a publisher for them. Apparently, she knew nothing about the publishing business and merely picked Peter Davies out of the telephone book. William Wall's first book, *Ringstones,* was published in 1951, a second, *The Sound of His Horn,* in 1952. All publications ceased with the poorly received *The Doll Maker,* and he always claimed that he had no further time for writing. The reality is that he wrote several unpublished books, including one in a private code consisting partly of shorthand and partly of Arabic. It has still to be deciphered. I do not doubt that someone will eventually bring the necessary energy and determination to this mysterious volume. There is, apparently, a sadistic and erotic element in much of his work, most notably (I have not read any of them) in *The King of the Lake,* a fable in which a crippled dwarf harnesses two women. He retired from the position of consul general in 1966 and died in 1989.

There are other possibilities. William Wall, a teacher, who left New York City to edit a company newsletter in Bangkok, Thailand, and whose close friend died in a climbing accident in Taiwan. The William Wall who erected a headstone to the memory of his father, the poet Eamon Wall, who died in Dungourney in 1763. The William Wall who was a colonial policeman, captured by the Japanese at Singapore, and whose brother remarked of him that he was the only man he ever heard of who was fatter coming out of a Japanese prison camp than he was going in. Or the William Wall mentioned by actor Cillian Murphy in a *Sunday Times* interview as having been a decent teacher. Or William Wall, a well-known citizen of Oswego Street, Camden Village, New York, claimed by pneumonia and buried on Tuesday, 27 January 1927. 'An Episcopalian, a very fine gentleman, friend and neighbor who will be greatly missed.' William Wall, who was born in Steeple Aston, Oxfordshire, England, who married Mary Plumb there, and who was buried there in 1812. He and Mary had twelve children, including a William who was born and died in Steeple Aston and whose burial is recorded for 1837. The William 'Silver Tip' Wall who was a member of Tom McCarty's gang and who briefly joined Butch Cassidy to rob the Denver and Rio Grande express near Grand Junction, Colorado, on 3 November 1887. The William Wall who wrote various Wisley Handbooks on bromeliads, begonias and African violets, and collaborated in 1996 with Clive Innes on *Cacti, Succulents and Bromeliads,* a Wisley Garden Companion. The William Wall who bequeathed divers lands and tenements, known as Wall's Lands, in the manor of Arlingham, to his son, who left them to Walter Wall who died in 1533. The William Wall who wrote *500 Ruy Lopez Miniatures* and other chess books. The Virginian William Wall who fought in Colonel Wood's and later Colonel Taylor's regiment of the Virginia Line during the American Revolutionary War. William Wall, Esq., of Coolnamuck, Waterford, who did not live to see his granddaughter Lucy marry John Harden of the City of Dublin on 15 April 1800 by special licence at Cork. The William Wall who wrote *Wake Up Dead* (Papillon Books/Aware Press, 1974), in which Tony Boyle, tough guy private eye, takes on a simple missing-person case only to find the case erupting 'into a volatile network of kidnapping, murder and bizarre danger'.

Fresher

'I remember it every day, every day. But I don't recall it. I mean not deliberately. That's what you are asking me to do now? You said: To recall the circumstances of the attack.'

'Certainly. I think it might be helpful.'

'You want me to start at the beginning?'

'Please.'

'Well, you know the details. I started last autumn, and you could say I was one of the greenest freshers on the campus. I mean, I believed in everything – all the crap about finding myself, the pursuit of truth and excellence, all the flimflam and gobbledegook they passed off on us. I swallowed it all. Major league.'

'Who passed this off on you?'

'Well, nobody exactly. It was sort of understood I suppose.'

'OK.'

'Plus, things like, I believed in the equality of the sexes. I believed boys and girls just want to have fun. It takes two to tango. Think of another cliché and I believed in it. I was super-naive. I was doing philosophy, and half the first term was taken up with a series of lectures about what they called the philosophical method – meaning how to extract the maximum amount of fluff from your own navel. We were supposed to dedicate ourselves to a minute examination of every assumption we ever made. Like, if I consider this tea hot, is it the tea in itself that is hot, or is it a perception, or what is the quality of hotness and how does it differ from the quality of coldness. Which is actually a big question, don't you think? Hotness as opposed to coldness? Being merely a psychologist, the profound nature of such speculations has probably escaped you.'

'On the contrary, quite a bit of psychology is made up of things like that.'

'Really? Tough luck. Anyway, I threw everything my mother ever told me out the window. God? Well, I suppose at that stage I just substituted a firm belief in atheism for a shaky belief in God. It was just this cool new religion. And now I don't give a damn whether God exists or not. I see it like this: If God exists he must be a right bastard to shag people the way he does. Forget about free will. If God exists he must know in advance what everybody is going to do, and what I want to know is, why doesn't he stop them. Not just rapists, but the soldiers and the bomber pilots. All of them. If God was even just half-human he'd stop them. You want to know what I think of God? God sucks. If there is a God, then the Devil must be equally powerful.'

'It's the Manichean heresy.'

'Really? Cool. Is that bad?'

'Very.'

'Anyway, I was a green fresher in college to pursue truth and excellence. I had it all – five As in my Leaving Cert. etc. All my relatives wanted to know why I didn't do Law instead of Arts. You know the way.

'Three weeks into term I discovered the Students' Union bar. I came from a small village where all the boys wanted to talk about was soccer and tractors. Occasionally they talked politics. I remember once being asked what kind of books I liked. I was stuck in a slow dance with a guy who thought my butt was something to practise massage on. He said, "Do you like books?

What kind of books do you like?" I told him the truth. "*The Second Sex* is a fantastic book," I said. This may sound strange to you but I just discovered it in the library. It knocked me out. "SEX?" he said, giving my left buttock a squeeze and trying to get his other hand inside my belt. I said it wasn't about sex, it was about The *Second* Sex. "Oh, women," he said. Bingo. QED.

'Anyway, that's where I came from. I expected real relationships in college; the boys I met there would want to share ideas, that kind of thing. And I wasn't against sex. In fact, in a relationship of equals . . . well, I don't need to spell it out. I saw no reason why I shouldn't sleep with someone if I loved him.

'This particular night I was with about eight other people. Some of them were from the next flat to mine, and my flatmate, Deirdre, was there too.

'*He* came in about ten o'clock. One of the other girls went out with him for a while, I think. Anyway, he latched on to me. And the truth is I was flattered. He wasn't exactly a hunk, but he was good-looking – tall and dark, a great talker too, and I discovered that he could talk philosophy as well as IT, which is what he was studying. I didn't notice that we were drinking a lot, or that he seemed to be slightly drunk when he arrived, although everyone else was able to tell me afterwards.

'At some stage we started kissing, and I realised that things had got on a bit. They started to flash the lights and shout *Time*. We all finished our drinks and agreed we'd go clubbing downtown, and then nearly everybody left, except him and Deirdre.

'When I got up, I was annoyed to find I was unsteady on my feet. I staggered if I didn't concentrate on what I was doing and my head kept jutting forward, so I was pleased when he put an arm around my shoulder. Deirdre kept asking me was I all right and I kept saying I was fine. I thought she was talking about being drunk, and I was getting snappy with her. In the end she stopped asking and just tagged along in silence. Now I know she was worried about him. She knew something that she never told me. She won't tell me now. When I asked him up to our flat, she said she'd see me later, that she was going on to the club, that I was to take care, and so on. The funny thing is, I couldn't get rid of her fast enough. As soon as she was gone, he started to kiss me in the hallway, and then inside the door of my flat. I suppose we had a pretty heavy session. You know the way.'

'Actually, I don't.'

'Well, I went farther with him than I ever did before. I was quite deliberate about it; it wasn't just the drink. I remember making a conscious decision. I let him undo my blouse and my bra and we spent about an hour kissing and touching, but I had made up my mind I was not going the whole way. I told him at one stage and he accepted it easily enough. I don't know if you can remember back that far, Dr Kane, but that kind of arrangement isn't unusual.'

'All right, carry on.'

'Anyway, about one o'clock we called it a night. I gave him a sleeping bag and got into bed myself, and pretty soon I was asleep. People do that all the time in college – boys in girls' rooms, girls in boys' rooms. It was probably different in your day. I remember looking forward to getting up in the morning and then I fell asleep. About an hour or so later, I woke up thinking I was choking, and he was on top of me. He was hurting me and threatening that if I made a sound he'd hit me. He kept telling me not to be a bitch. I didn't put up much of a struggle, as you know from the doctor's report, and anyway it was all over fairly quickly. He seemed to think there was nothing wrong and was quite nice about it before he fell asleep. He thought I was crying because I had lost my virginity.'

'And it was really because . . .'

'I was crying because I was disgusted. Wasted. I felt filthy, and terrified that he might wake up again. Most of all I felt out of control. It was my body – not a toy. It's not too much to ask – to be able to say no about something important. Is it?'

'One would think not.'

'And he accepted it at the time I told him. He seemed to just go to sleep. He made a fool out of me and then he used me.

'Well, as soon as he started to snore, I got up and washed. I couldn't wash enough. I remember thinking about Lady Macbeth, you know, *Out, damned spot?* We did that for the Leaving. But it wouldn't come out, the spot. Nothing would ever get it out. It was inside me and belonged to me. It was mine now. He gave it to me. He put it into me.

'That was when Deirdre got back. I told her the whole story, and she was almost more upset than I was. She wanted to call the guards, but I wouldn't let her. I didn't want to go through all that stuff about court appearances and tests and everything. I didn't want anything like that, which when you think about why I'm here is pretty funny. Anyway, she agreed.

'Then, typical students, we decided we'd have a cup of tea. Can you believe that? After being raped? It couldn't happen in New York!

'Deirdre put the kettle on, and I went and washed again, and when I came back she was gone. She was only gone in next door to see if anyone had Panadol, because I told her I was sore, but I got a bad shock. The kettle was boiling fast, building up pitch, and I was standing there in a pyjamas with a rapist snoring next door. I suppose that's when it happened. I didn't even think about it. I just picked the kettle up and walked in. He was lying flat on his back with one arm behind his head; probably he was settling in better now that I was out of the bed and he had it all to himself.

'Anyway, I raised the quilt from the bottom and folded it over his stomach and then I poured the boiling water over his genitals. Did you ever kill ants with boiling water? My mother used to get me to do it. You know, just before they fly? You'd see swarms of them coming out of cracks in the yard. It was like that. My standing there swinging the kettle over him.

'The thought of purification came into my head. You asked me before what I was thinking, and I wasn't thinking anything really. Not thoughts, organised and so on. I remember thinking that it was like when they pour water over a baby's head to baptise him and the original sin is just wiped away as if it never existed. *A little water clears us of this deed*, to quote Lady M again. I suppose the idea of boiling something to sterilise it was in my mind, too.

'Anyway, it had an incredible effect. After maybe two seconds he jumped almost straight up, like someone had plugged him into a thousand volts. He started shouting, screaming really, and fell on his face clutching his thing. What was left of it. I think he passed out. There was a strange kind of smell – boiled chicken and sex. And a wet place in the bed.

'Deirdre came rushing in, and as soon as she saw what happened she rang for an ambulance, and within minutes they were all over the place. I remember Deirdre saying, 'He raped my friend,' and I burst into tears when she said *friend*. I don't know why. She said it several times and each time I cried. I felt ridiculous.'

'Did you feel any remorse?'

'No.'

'Did you think you could get away with it? Did you think they wouldn't bring you before the courts? That something like that could go unpunished?'

'No.'

'What did you feel when they told you about the damage you had inflicted?'

'Will I tell you? You probably won't believe it. The first thing I thought of was that smell and how I would never be able to face a cooked chicken again. Would you believe that? And when they left, I went back to bed. I slept like a lamb until they came for me the next day.'

'And?'

'And the trouble is I haven't been able to sleep much since. I don't know why. Remember – he raped me first.'

In the Egyptian Collection

The guards are on strike, but they have agreed to open one door each hour. At the end of that hour, the floor is closed and all visitors must descend by the stairs. I want to see the collection from Pompeii and Herculaneum but end up in the basement looking at the dead Egyptians and their ornaments. Everybody else is taking photographs despite the signs, but I don't want to remember anything so I look away. But every now and then, embarrassment makes me turn around. You can't keep admiring the way the sunlight comes through the blinds or saying how cool it is after the heat outside. It's August in Naples and they're having a heatwave, which means it must be forty-three or -four and the air-conditioning on the bus didn't work properly, and a man was smoking. 'Oh my God, look at this,' someone says. 'It's a hand.' I look because not to look would draw attention to me, and in a glass case there is a child's hand slipped out from the brown wrapping. 'I think mummies are disgusting,' my friend Marie says. I don't. I think they're too sad to look at. The others are all wondering what they died of, and what colour hair and eyes they had, and whether they were sacrificed or something. And right this minute, in some village in England, people are looking at graves and wondering the same thing about other little girls, people bussed in to look, so we can make a profit even out of people dying. I think that's disgusting. I think we'll all end up in hell, whatever hell is. Maybe this little girl all wrapped up and half-rotten and lying in a glass case is in hell. Maybe that's what's in store for people who look at dead bodies and try to pretend that they're sad for the dead people when they're really not sad at all. I said to Marie, 'I'm getting out of here,' and she said, 'You can't. You have to descend by the stairs, and the stairs is closed because of the strike until the end of the hour.' And I try the doors and they're locked. 'Oh Jesus. We are all stuck in the basement. What about a fire, Marie?' I can see it as if it is really happening – the bars on the windows red like the elements in an electric heater, the blinds in flitters, the glass cases all exploding. There is even a man smoking. He probably feels safe because the guards are on strike, and no one has the courage to tell him stop, and we're locked in so nobody will see him. He smoked all the way up in the bus, even though the sign said no smoking and I couldn't breathe. I told Marie I thought I'd have to be sick, but she said to get a grip on myself, which I just managed to do, but I don't know how I'll stick it going back. I'll have to ask to sit in the front near the driver because he has a window open. Mummies are embalmed, and I happen to know that embalming involves alcohol which burns with a very clear flame, like the flame on the top of Christmas pudding. My father used to light it, and he always said what a waste, all this good whiskey going up in smoke, and he used to pretend to blow it out too early so the whiskey would get a chance to soak into the pudding, and my mother would get cross. He's an accountant and doesn't like waste. In an hour we would all burn very clear. That man who smokes has a lighter that he often clicks and lets it out again, a silver or steel lighter. Sometimes I hear the click but I don't see the flame. Marie says, 'Look at all these little toys, little men and insects and animals, all perfect. Imagine, all those years and they still come out of the ground perfect. Who'd think that they could make things as small so long ago.' Perfect is her favourite word. The hotel was perfect and some fellow that she set her heart on and a T-shirt she bought. 'Maybe they belonged to the little girl,' she says, 'the toys.' Marie only half-reads the notices and so she doesn't know that all the toys were discovered in different places at different times, but I don't tell her. I know from experience that it's a waste of time telling her anything. The English in the signs is funny, and some of the signs are only in Italian. You can see that the English ones are translated. What language did the little girl speak? I don't think it's what they speak over there now. I think her language is dead, too. I think that's too sad. Even if I wanted to comfort her and find a quiet moment when everyone else was looking at the jewellery, I couldn't do it because the right words don't exist any more anywhere, not even a language I could study and maybe get a phrasebook in, like the Italian one I have. But then I remember that even babies respond to tone of voice. Where did I hear that? On a radio show I suppose, where I hear everything, some talk show. When I heard that, it upset me because of what I did at that time, as if I had any choice. If I could make my voice soothing enough, she'd understand that I wanted her to feel happy. After a few thousand years, I might be the first voice she heard that cared for her. Since her mother said goodbye and she was put in that dark cold tomb. Even in Egypt tombs have to be cold. And the people who found her would have been excited, the archaeologists. They would have called her a find, not a little girl. I don't think anyone would have thought about how she felt. So I wait for a bit until the crowd moves on and Marie says, 'Aren't you coming?' And I say 'No, I'm not interested. I'm staying here.' She gives me a look. It hasn't been a success, coming with Marie, and I won't do it again. She's only interested in one thing. So she goes with the others, and I hear their voices oohing and aahing about the gold and stuff. I can imagine what it looks like. And I stay and talk to the little girl. And after about three minutes I'm crying. 'I have a little sister just like you,' I say. 'Just like you. And I miss her.' I don't know what I'm going to do because I can't go back. I told them I'd never go back after what they said. My father writes to me but my mother doesn't. She's very black about it. 'You walk out that door, my lassie, and you won't walk back,' she said. My mother. 'You'll be as the dead to me,' she said. And so I am. It's getting cold down here now, like the air-conditioning is turned down too far. I want to put my hand through the glass and cover up the little hand which is the only part you can see except for the toes of one foot. It's like she's asleep and has pulled the blankets up around herself and turned over on to her back and her hand is sticking out and her toes too. But it's the hand I want to cover. Hands tell you everything. It's the hand that carries the lifeline that shows with branching and forking what things are going to happen, even though we're better off not knowing the future, it's all there if we knew how to read it. And when we want to help someone, we say we'll lend them a hand or give them a hand up, and when we're getting rid of something we say, I'll hand it over to you, it's all in your hands, it's out of my hands now. I wash my hands of it. And you can tell a person's work by her hands, like mine are always red and sort of raw-looking because I'm allergic to the rubber gloves they make us wear in the factory. We have to wear plastic hats, too, and surgeons' masks and gowns like we're operating on people instead of computers: like all the chips and boards we fit together are parts of people who will wake up after a long sleep and their lives will be better and maybe they'll be able to walk again and not have any pain. My father is waiting on a plastic-hip operation, but these things have to be ripe, his doctor says, and he'll have a long wait yet. And all we're doing is putting modems together, and Marie is the only one who can afford a computer, so none of us girls even knows how they work. 'So what am I going to do?' I ask the little girl. I brush the hair off her face, the way I do my sister's. In my mind's eye I see us: me sitting beside her bed which is not this cold glass cabinet but an ordinary bed like we have at home, and I brush the hair out of her eyes. What am I going to do at all, I'll never see them again? Then Marie comes back. 'Sweet Jesus, this is meant to be an effing holiday,' she says. 'Look at you. Jesus.' 'It's none of your business,' I say. 'And it's not much of a holiday, is it?' 'You booked it,' she says. 'You wanted a cultural tour when we could've been in Crete or the Canaries. Jesus wept.' So I tell her there and then. 'I'm walking out that door,' I say, 'as soon as the hour is up, and if I never see you again I'll be just as happy. And I'm asking the supervisor to change my station when I get back. If I never talk to you again I'll be just as happy. And if you want to know, this little girl reminds me of my sister.' 'Sweet Jesus,' Marie says. 'How could she remind you of your sister. You make me sick.' And she's looking at the glass case, and I know all she can see is something dead. No, something that was never alive, like one of the toys or the statues or like the little girl was stillborn instead of being ten or eleven years old. 'When a child dies before it's born, she was never alive,' I say. 'And so she could never die. It's what limbo means.' 'You lost it completely now,' Marie says. 'What in Christ's name are you talking about now?' 'You're the kind of person who reads all the horror stories,' I say, 'like those two little girls in England. You love that.' She stares at me. 'What are you talking about? What girls?' But I hear the guards opening the door and there's a gust of warm air and they're looking at us like they just found out we're down here. 'It's ascend,' I say. 'You have to ascend by the stairs. You're in the basement now. If you want to get out you have to go up.' And I just walk away.

Dionysus and the Titans

'There . . . near the sacred tripod on which the Pythia sat to
prophesy, was to be seen a strange object – a sort of coffin or
cinerary urn with the inscription, Here lieth the body of Dionysus,
the son of Semele.'

Walter Pater – *Greek Essays*

Semele drove too fast, and coming round the tight corner a
mile from the hotel, the car ploughed into a buck-rake
attached at an angle to the back of a tractor. The manner of the
accident had this virtue, that she probably never knew what was
happening, unless the brain retains a thought during the time
when the mouth opens and closes by nervous instinct. Probably
Semele just died. However, her body nurtured Denis long
enough for the police to call the firemen to cut away the buck-
rake and the parts of the car that had imprisoned her legs, and
for the fireman with the cutting torch to notice that she was
pregnant and apparently in labour. So they ventilated Semele
and let nature take its course otherwise, and that was how Denis
presented to this world, a brown-skinned baby in the intermit-
tent light of the police cars, the faint blue glow of the cutting
torch. An inauspicious beginning.

'That was Semele that was,' the fireman with the cutting
torch said. 'Jesus, she was one beauty.'

The sergeant of the police said, 'Get that bastard Zoot. He's probably in the hotel.' And a car sped off around the bend that Semele had missed and came back with Zoot, blind drunk as usual, but sober enough to know that his lover had presented him with a problem.

'This is the last straw,' he said. He took a look at the baby, and then he stuck his head into the car and looked at Semele. After that he had seen enough. He took the baby and walked off into the night.

'That bates all,' the fireman said. He watched Zoot flickering on and off in the revolving lights, and then he turned to someone else and said, 'Better get the Social Services in on this. That bastard Zoot'll kill the child.'

'I'm going to call him Denis,' Zoot said, turning at the edge of the light. 'After my father.'

The firemen and policemen snickered because they all knew that the identity of Zoot's father was a mystery, but they hid their snickering from Zoot because, after all, it was a small place and everyone had to live together somehow.

So Zoot settled down a bit, drinking less, playing poker only once a week, working occasionally while still signing on, milking the government whenever possible and benefiting from time to time from various schemes devised to please bureaucrats and extract money from them. The Social Services got involved and did their best to get Zoot to give the child up without a fight.

They started by trying to undermine his self-confidence. 'Zoot,' they said, 'you can't raise a child. What do you know about children? You've been drinking since you were what? Ten? Twelve?'

'Nine,' Zoot said sourly. Once that was a boast, now, plainly, it was going to become a liability, but it did not occur to Zoot to lie.

'You smoke like a trooper. Untipped too.'

Zoot put on his mournful look which was such a favourite with women. The Social Services was a woman. 'I'm giving them up for Lent.'

'Lent is six months away. You're out every night in one pub or another. You and Semele weren't married. You'd be a bad example to the child.'

'I mostly go to the hotel now,' Zoot said defensively.

'And another thing, Denis is coloured. How are you going to raise a coloured child in a place like this? He'll stick out like a sore thumb.'

'That's because of Semele,' he said. 'Semele was West Indian. There's no coloured blood on my side.'

'For God's sake, don't lecture me on genetics,' the woman said. 'What I'm saying is, it isn't right.'

Zoot saw a glimmer of light there, an opportunity. 'That's a racist remark,' he said. 'I could complain you for that. They'd show you the door.'

The Social Services sighed. 'I'm going to watch you like a hawk,' she said. 'You haven't seen the last of me.'

Zoot lived in one of those labourer's cottages that the government put up around 1930. It belonged to his grandfather, and when his grandfather went soft in the head and Zoot put him in the County Home, he more or less inherited it at a nominal rent, except that it still belonged to the Council. His grandfather, whose father remembered the famine, was careful to grow a mixture of vegetables and potatoes on the acre of land that came with the cottage. He grew carrots and cabbage and turnips and sometimes French beans, which looked like a spattering of blood on eight-foot canes when they were in flower. He also grew potatoes, which he regarded with suspicion because of his father's stories of Black '47. But when Zoot put him in the Home, the vegetables went to seed and rotted, and nature reclaimed the garden. Zoot and Semele used to make love down there on summer nights, protected from the world by a sub-tropical cabbage forest.

At the age of seventy-four, the old man set fire to a wooden shed and burned his legs when the paint tins started to explode. Although he recovered well from the burns, he rambled in his head. On one occasion, he made tea with rat poison. On another he tried to make a giant flute out of a piece of downpipe. Zoot called in the doctor, and they agreed that he was a danger to himself and to others, so they took him to the County Home and left him in a pair of striped pyjamas in a bed with an iron frame. The last words Zoot heard him say were, 'I never thought I'd finish up in the poorhouse.'

Zoot came back a week later to see how the old man was settling in and was met at the door of the ward by a dusky nurse who told him, in a curious sing-song accent, that his father was depressed. Zoot did not understand a word she said, but he was fascinated by the curious articulation of breasts and hips and the relationship between her uniform and her thighs. The fact that his grandfather sat staring at him for thirteen minutes by his bedside alarm clock without uttering a single word made no impression on him. Before he left he had invited her for a drink. She was Semele. She moved into the cottage a month later.

It was a useful arrangement because Semele earned enough to satisfy Zoot's food requirements, and he generally had enough to spend on beer himself. He never drank spirits because, he said, shorts were for alkies. But Semele appreciated a good lover, and Zoot was one of that rare breed that seek pleasure for themselves only through giving pleasure to others. He was the first man in Ireland to give Semele an orgasm, and once he had got the hang of it, he racked up an impressive total of seven at one sitting. 'You got to be the most *exhausting*, boy,' she would say to him, full of languid admiration. 'The *best*.' Zoot grew in her admiration and became an expert in the field. He could have given courses in love if only Brussels would recognise it as a valid subject for grant aid. Which they do not.

So, in a way protected from tragedy by the fact that she got more out of him than he got out of her, Zoot was largely unaffected by Semele's death. The way he saw it, it was her loss more than his. After all, *he* was still alive.

The baby was a different matter though. Given time, selfishness would have corroded the fragile bond of father and son, and Denis would have turned up on the front step of a police station wrapped in army-surplus blankets. Time alone could have effected this alteration without the necessity of any other stimulus, because Zoot would simply have got bored. But Social Services would condemn him equally for abandoning the baby and holding on to it. The only correct course was to transfer care of the child to them in an orderly fashion, according to procedure. But here Zoot's innate resentment of an organisation that frequently questioned whether he was really available for work came into play. When they disputed his right to keep the child, he asserted his paternity. When they said he couldn't care for a child, he took a parenting course. When they said the house wasn't fit for human habitation (there was no glass in two windows, for example, since a night when Zoot had called Semele a black cunt), he organised a Council grant for refurbishment and employed a builder to put in a shower, replace all the wooden windows with PVC double-glazed and build a porch outside the front door to keep out the draft. He learned to coo and change nappies and talk baby talk. He never slept a full night and complained to the ladies that he wished he had tits because it would make life easier.

To defeat the system, he became a perfect parent.

A curious side effect was that he became attached to the child.

The Social Services did not give up for three years, and during that time, as Denis slowly became a boy instead of a child, Zoot made the struggle into a game. 'The SS are coming,' he would shout and walk stiff-legged around the room, stretching his arm at an angle to his body. Sometimes he would paint on a false moustache, and on those occasions he would look very like Charlie Chaplin playing Adenoid Hynkler in *The Great Dictator*, because Zoot was very small and narrow shouldered as a result of getting his nourishment out of a tap for most of his life. He did have a neat, round beer belly though, which Semele used to find irresistible.

As Denis got older, he came to love this game and would ask for it often, especially before going to bed, and Zoot built a whole mythology around it. He told Denis of the Bogey SS-woman who stole children and ate them, of the Giant SS-woman who turned children into slaves, of the SS Inspector who closed down public houses and herded up fathers who were drinking after hours, of the SS-Storm Troopers who came on windy nights and rattled the doors and windows and made moaning noises in the chimney. But along with the stories, Zoot imbued Denis with a strong feeling of security. 'Look what Daddy did,' he would say. 'He put in unbreakable double glazing. The Storm Troopers can't break that.' He told great lies of battles with the SS and one true story about how he had escaped over the back wall of Mack's pub when the place was raided an hour after closing time. And Denis grew up happy and natural until he was three years of age and Zoot made a fatal mistake that the parenting course should have prevented but didn't because people who give courses like that have no concept of history.

Zoot decided to celebrate Denis's third birthday in style, and since three was a considerable age, he believed it was time to bring in a babysitter. Being a careful father he cast around for a suitable person to do the job. Simon and Anna Tynan were his cousins, so he felt he knew them well enough, despite the fact that he had never spoken to them before except at his grandfather's funeral when they said, 'I'm sorry for your trouble,' and he replied, 'Thanks a lot.'

The Tynans were as tall as Zoot was short and were so alike, with the same thin white face and staring eyes, that people thought they were twins instead of just brother and sister. They were almost the same age as Zoot and had never worked a day in their lives either. However, they had watched parents at work on children, and when Zoot phoned them from the hotel, they rubbed their hands together in glee and set about acquiring a repertoire of amusing behaviour. They bought a pair of Punch and Judy hand puppets, a doll's mirror and a rattle. They arrived ten minutes early and watched Zoot shaving himself at the kitchen sink with some interest. When Zoot said he would be back by closing time, they said, 'Take your time. No rush.'

Zoot thought of them as the perfect babysitters all the way to the hotel. Then he thought of a pint of Murphy's.

He came home blind drunk at two o'clock in the morning, having had the benefit of the residents' lounge and the company of the night porter/owner until that time. He found the Social Services waiting, the Tynans side by side on the couch and Denis asleep across their laps holding the rattle and one of the puppets. It was a shock to his system, and he had to turn around again and vomit into the undergrowth of the cabbage patch. But vomiting didn't clear his head, which is probably why he bit the Social Services woman and tried to strangle Simon Tynan. But Anna Tynan overpowered him, and uttering some kind of weird mantra, they withdrew, taking Denis with them. The last out the door was the Social Services who gave him a withering look and said, 'We'll be getting a care order. I warned you.'

So by means of a convoluted legal process, Zoot lost Denis to the system. There were numerous court appearances, during which the Social Services proved to have a very long memory and rich and varied sources of information, and Zoot was surprised by the number of things he had done in his short life. Once, in a happier mood, he was heard to remark that he didn't realise he was such a hellraiser.

For the duration of the process, Denis was given into foster care, for which the Tynans were a natural choice. They won the child over easily with the Punch and Judy show and the rattle because Zoot had never bought toys of any kind. People said it was a pity they didn't get out and about more, the Tynans, and find someone to marry because they were such lovely people and it wasn't natural for a brother and sister to live together in such harmony. Mothers came to advise about childcare, and it was rumoured that Anna was going to do the same parenting course that Zoot had done years before. Even the Social Services were pleased with the arrangement. So it came as a tremendous shock when Simon and Anna Tynan cooked Denis and were so foolish as to offer a neighbour a kind of shepherd's pie which contained what was plainly a brown penis, although they tried to pass it off as sausage.

When the police arrested them, the only part that remained, besides the penis, was Denis's heart, all frosted and white in the deep freeze. The Chief State Pathologist examined them, and they were entered as evidence in the trial. Later the penis was thrown out in error, but the heart was carefully preserved.

Zoot was in the hotel the day the heart came back, and when he saw the box in the sergeant's hands, he knew what it was. 'Don't tell me they're going to charge the full whack for this,' he said. 'It's only a heart.' But the parish wouldn't sell him a six-inch grave, and he had to go to the Social Services for the money to bury Denis. The Tynans got life.

Periastron

We went out to the garden to send the dog on his late-night neighbourliness. It had been blowing a gale for two or three days, but last night everything was completely still. There was a very fine layer of cloud that made a glory round the moon. It blanked out most of the stars except for Mars, which was burning through brighter than ever.

She said, 'It's the closest it's been in sixty thousand years.' We looked a long time at it.

Then this morning, when I woke, I knew immediately that everything was different. It was not that she wasn't moving or that I could not hear her breathing. The room seemed to have set like a jelly. What was becoming was over. Heraclitus said: *Awake we share the same world, but the sleeper turns away into a world of his own.* I will spare you the horror of shaking and calling and naming; the grief, the shock, the self-loathing and, most of all, the self-interest. You can well imagine the almost comic panic that overtook me.

What I would like to do now is to consider that simple juxtaposition. Last night we looked at Mars together, a moment of intimacy of the kind that is thought to give meaning to a life, or at least to relationships within that life. I don't know how long we stood there, but certainly it was nothing when compared to the long return journey of the planet.

It was a warm night. The frontal system that brought the wind brought warmth, too, and in sheltered places it was this that one remarked. I remember Carla wore a green cardigan, but she hadn't bothered to button it up. I myself was in shirt-sleeves. Before coming out we had been listening to Mozart, as we often did before going to bed, and the strains of 'Porgi, amor' could be heard very faintly through the partly open French doors. So faintly that if I did not know what was playing, I perhaps would not have been able to say what it was, but knowing that the turn of the little cavatina had come round, I was acutely aware of the sentiments. *Give me love or let me die.* The coincidence is risible.

Leaves lit the lawn, scattered by the equinoctial gales that I remember so well from when I was a boy. They would come thundering up the bay and expend themselves in impotent fury against the stone quay and the wall. Occasionally, aided by certain circumstances – extremely low pressure, a south-easterly set in the wind, a fresh in the river – they would penetrate the village via the sewer pipes, and then all kinds of malign forms would present. Once my grandmother saw four rats emerge from her toilet bowl. It caused her angina. Bowel movements would return mysteriously like a colossal dyspepsia.

Clara's father was a mathematician, on the other hand, and she grew up in the immaculate atmosphere of pure forms. I don't think she ever saw a rat, much less knew what direction the wind blew from, but she was conversant with number theory by the time she was old enough to dance at the club. She played tennis and wore frocks. Her father's signature had three initials. He was tall and thin and pale in the Protestant way. Had we not found ourselves at the same university, we would certainly never have met, our worlds were so different.

We identified Mars easily enough. It was the brightest thing in the heavens at the time, and anyway it was the only real light besides the moon. The moon herself was wound in concentric circles of primary colours.

I said, 'I'm trying to think of the word for it, when two planets are at their closest. It's not periastron, is it?'

'Whatever,' she said.

The dog returned.

It was the pattern of every night. Nothing exceptional gave us pause, unless her remark about the length of time it had taken Mars to approach. We did not touch. It would have been out of place.

This morning then I phoned for the doctor.

Like everyone else, I believed I understood something about friendship. Like everyone else, I believed I was living my own version of hell, purgatory or paradise at various times of my life. Like everyone else, I believed in, or felt, the celebrated numinous union that is supposed to exist between two people who have spent a decade or two in each other's company. Afterwards, I was inclined to defend it – because of the terrible waste.

False, of course. From both points of view. An elaborate conceit. And nature is not wasteful.

Carla said, 'It's the closest it's been in sixty thousand years.'

And I said, 'It *is* very bright.'

I thought, or said – I'm not sure which – that I hadn't noticed its approach.

The dog returned and went indoors, sliding the door open first with the tip of his nose, then with his whole head, a finesse that has polished the aluminium at twelve inches high.

And this morning I told the doctor she was certainly dead.

Had I checked for a pulse?

'No need.'

I heard the irritation. I expected him to say that for a scientist I am very cavalier about data, but he did not. We have grown old together and have learned to be tolerant. He told me that he would come as soon as possible. Then, almost as an afterthought, he told me that he was sorry. I thanked him and hung up.

Almost immediately the doorbell rang. It was my neighbour complaining that the dog had been using his garden again. I apologised but he did not want to go away. This is not the first time, as I must know; he has kept a list of complaints; he has had enough. He referred to the shits as *nuisances*. My dog is leaving his nuisances on his lawn. It has a legal ring to it. I apologised again. He asked me what I was going to do about it.

I said I couldn't really think about it just then because my wife had died.

At first he seemed about to laugh. Then he reconsidered and arranged his face into a show of sorrow. He said if that were true he was very sorry to disturb me.

I said it was quite true. I asked him to verify the fact for himself by coming upstairs and checking her pulse. He was about to agree then changed his mind. He left.

I went upstairs myself and sat on her side of the bed. There was a curious woodenness to her weight. It was as though the body had already renounced possibility and was beginning to compose itself in some permanent state, a proposition that ran counter to the biological facts, and seemed at the time to carry a spiritual freight as well. Her face had taken on a kind of vitreous beauty that would have pleased her, her skin pale and clear and firm, and the dark Italian eyebrows, straight as rules, that she inherited from the grandmother after whom she was named. She had not opened her eyes.

When he came to the door a second time, I was making coffee and had no option but to invite him in or seem rude, standing at the door with the cafetière in my hand. I lifted it and shook it slightly at him, in what I hoped was an inviting rather than a threatening manner, and he followed me into the kitchen. I suspected, I don't know why, that he had known in advance that I was making breakfast and that he deliberately chose that moment to knock in the hope of joining me.

We sat in the kitchen drinking coffee and eating biscuits – I did not have the energy or the concentration to cook anything and I was very hungry. I told him about Mars and that Carla had read something about it, and he seemed interested. I said I had been trying to think about the sixty thousand years it had taken Mars and Earth to get so close. I told him that next year would have been our fortieth anniversary. I said that unexpected death is a pitiless irony, coming, as it does, when time has brought people closer than ever. Almost immediately I regretted putting that thought in words. He asked me questions about her interests. Did she follow my own scientific bent? What kind of physical activities did she enjoy? He had, apparently, seen her once or twice at the tennis club. Did she like cooking? None of his questions seemed relevant in any way, nor did they appear to be leading in any direction. It did not seem like any kind of an inquisition, and I was unable to decide whether he suspected me of murder or merely wanted to make a nuisance of himself. I think we finished an entire packet of water biscuits, because later in the day I could not find any. I thought it strange to be chatting amiably to a man with whom I had fought the dog war for three years. I had barely saluted him during that time.

Then the doctor arrived and my neighbour left in haste. He seemed embarrassed to have taken up my time. Even the doctor noticed it.

'What bit him?' he said.

He stood in the hall a moment and watched him go down the drive. Then he turned and shook my hand.

'Now, let's see what we can do,' he said.

But, of course, there was nothing he could do, although he took charge of making the necessary phone calls.

'Poor dear Carla,' he said. 'Still, Eric, you know, she died peacefully in her sleep. It's a blessed way to go. Please God we'll all slip away so easy.'

I cannot now express the anger I felt at these words. I said nothing, of course. I recognise a curious state of detachment that I have heard overtakes the bereaved. We experience things as being done to us, passively, rather than actively directing our own emotions. We can even observe our own behaviour in an almost scientific way. The world, on the other hand, is a muffled thing, a limited register of sensory perceptions. I was able to thank him courteously and show him to the door, but when he left, I had to sit down and make a deliberate effort to master my emotions.

Since then no one has called. Naturally the undertakers are inefficient. I have phoned twice, and on each occasion I have been infuriated by the unctuous voice, by the laughable excuses, chief of which is that they are under extreme pressure because of the flu. Whether they are short-staffed because of sick leave or snowed under with corpses is something I have not bothered to clarify. However, the day has passed and a wintry evening is setting in.

What Slim Boy, O Pyrrha

I give you the image of a man running naked into battle. Not quite naked, because he wears his helmet. Why do we feel he is peculiarly vulnerable? As if his uniform of coarse cloth could protect him against a high-velocity rifle-round or a stream of bullets from a Maxim gun. The period, of course, is 1914–1918 – the Maxim gun is the key. Is he an officer or a private soldier? And why is he naked?

Say, his trench has been surprised during the night, and now that the initial raid has been repulsed, he leads his men in a counter-attack. '*Carpe diem!*' he shouts to them, although they do not understand the language. '*Carpe diem.*' He has a battered copy of Horace's *Odes* (Everyman Library Edition) in his kit. He waves his revolver above his head, and they grin and say the old man has finally gone bats.

The image has certain engaging qualities: a naked man (under the mushroom cap of his helmet) stands on the lip of a trench and urges his men to attack, in Latin. But they follow him because he is the old man, because he talks to them in some foreign lingo, because he's starkers and he doesn't give a tuppenny damn. They pour over the trench, chuckling affectionately, and into the brilliant artificial day of no man's land, and the bullets fly and the star-shells pop and hiss. The men hear the bullets that do not have their names on them whispering suddenly in the air, but nobody hears the bullet that has his name. It nips the jugular, holes the aorta, or slips in above the ear and exits into the helmet set at a jaunty angle, filling it with brain.

At some time in the half-hour of this particular battle, the naked officer stands above the corpse of a German soldier who has been shot through the eye. Another distressing image. A bullet in the eye is a barbarous wound. The naked man looks down at the one-eyed un-seer.

Now that his sexual organs have come into our field of view, the issue of his sleeping naked arises. It is well known that officers in the front-line trenches slept in their uniforms. We are familiar with descriptions of the damp dugouts, lit by a single candle, full of the thunder of the cannonade, in which sensitive and insensitive men of various ages sit about or doze, in uniforms of various ranks, the highest usually being a major. The officer who packs Horace's *Odes* before leaving Blighty is also a familiar figure. He may well have started the war with *Odi profanum vulgus,* but will end it, if he survives, with *occidit occidit spes omnis*. The *vulgus* will become closer to him than the people of his own class, and he will emerge into Civvy Street a hopeless misfit or a revolutionary. He inspires fierce loyalty among his men, who refer to him by various insulting names which are, in fact, terms of endearment, such as 'The Old Man' or 'Mad Harry'.

But this beats all. Even his batman is shocked by his appearance on the lips of the trench. They are all looking up at him, and from that angle he is an impressive figure, almost sculpted in the heroic mode. He might have graced a pedestal in Rome or Athens. Various comments about his genitalia (Are they large or small? Something to come back to later if we have time) that pass along the sap in the few moments before they realise the mad bugger wants them to counter-attack are silenced by the non-commissioned officers.

But now to explain his nakedness necessitates a deliberate switch in time. We consider the possibility of a nostalgic passage encapsulating the memory of an incident which led him into this aberration and realise immediately (or after a few hundred words) that the effect will be to slow the narrative without adding in any way to the suspense. Nor can he reasonably be expected to begin telling someone a sub-narrative at the height of an attack. This is a story, and devices available to novelists – interleaving chapters in a complex time-frame, for example – are not appropriate here. In the end, because I want to get on with it, I type three asterisks and go straight into his memory of the day he said goodbye to a certain woman in Beaulieu (it is pronounced *Bewley*, and, surprisingly, is in the south of England, not France) on a languid summer afternoon in 1914.

* * *

The sun is low on the evening of a perfect day. The cypress trees cast long irregular shadows on the manicured lawn. In the distance, the pock of mallet and ball can be heard. (Or perhaps the pock of bat and ball? The villagers have come to the house of the rich man – the lord? – for their annual cricket match against the tenants. They linger in the edge of memory, in white, doing very little for long periods and then rushing about in inexplicable patterns. The whirling arm, the swing of the bat – pock.) Down the cypress walk you go, from shadow to shadow, following the woman and the man. You hear their tender conversation. He wears the uniform of the Hampshire Regiment, and with a gasp you realise that this is the first time in the story that you have seen him with his clothes on. It creates a peculiar kind of intimacy which you find contradictory. At first you see them at a distance, moving elegantly among the trees. Then you approach more closely, and finally you are a secret third party to their conversation, the ghost of the future standing with them, shoulder to shoulder.

It comes as a shock to discover that their conversation is salty and sexual. They are reliving an actual sexual encounter in detail. The language they use is pure D.H. Lawrence. Because you are a ghost, you are privy also to the man's actual thoughts, and I have given him certain phrases from Catullus and Ovid (we have already established that he is a classicist) which confirm the universality of the terms. But her thoughts are out of bounds because it suits the direction of the narrative to have an inscrutable heroine. She is always other in the story, an object of his thoughts, his memories, his fantasies. And yours. After a time the subtle interplay of the still, warm evening, the gentle sound of the cricket game, the sex and the Latin, create an extraordinary sensuality, a Mediterranean languor set against the battlefield images with which the story opened. Now the felicity of that switch (indicated merely by three asterisks) becomes clear. And because we have really moved in time – rather than merely moving into memory – the detail can be piled up to add to the overall effect. What do they look like? She is tall and slim and moves with a fluid grace. He is taller, thin because he is a scholar, with the stiff back of the stoic (or the officer). He thinks poetically, seamlessly, in several languages, but he speaks haltingly. His words are clipped, uncertain, hesitant. His accent is Anglo-Irish, hers is Swiss finishing school via Chesterfield Ladies' College. When he is required to utter complete sentences, he stutters as though he is aware that he is a foreigner in several tongues. He loves her madly, of course. At least this is the way he thinks of it, the precise phrase in fact. When he is away from her, he dreams constantly of her body and certain parts of it in particular. Now, as he walks, he moves his hand to his face and smells her on it, and she laughs because this is a shared joke. She knows where his hand has been. Even at the dinner table, or at stilted gatherings in her father's drawing room, or in a railway carriage, he only has to make the shadow of the same gesture and she smiles. We know she likes to use the most vulgar terms for parts of his body and hers, the coarseness itself exciting her – her face is a little flushed now – and all of this is somehow related, in an extraordinary way, to her elegance and refinement.

They walk side by side but not arm in arm, because there is something that prevents them from being seen as a couple. In fact, there are two things. Firstly, of course, she is the daughter of a lord, a millionaire who has made his money in the shipping business and now sails a yacht in the same races as King George and the Kaiser. On the other hand, *he* comes from a middle-class family of university teachers, clergymen and scholars. His family may construct the way England thinks (a hundred years before, Ireland too), but England, or at least its rich, use the construction to ignore or despise anybody who thinks at all. Her father has envisioned a marriage of alliance for her, with the son of a man who owns, among other things, a commercial insurance company.

The second impediment is a more subtle one: they are cousins. The term *scion* is appropriate but vastly overused in relation to the English nobility, a metaphor drawn from the practice of grafting plants and redolent of a certain vegetable quality in that class. Equally, the term *distaff side,* a metaphor drawn from the manufacture of clothing at cottage industry level, is not entirely appropriate. I leave the construction of the relationship for the rewrite. Suffice it to say that he is from the Irish branch of the family which labours under some disgrace incurred during the eighteenth century and which the stern and dour behaviour of six or seven generations has not been sufficient to erase.

They are cousins and therefore the odour of incest permeates their bed. This is an inappropriate and an illegitimate relationship and is therefore doomed.

At this point you realise that the young man will die.

He can never return to find his lover married to a boring fart who drives a Bugatti or a private aeroplane. She would be miserable, and he would feel futile. A tragic as opposed to a depressing ending has become a necessity. When we last saw him in the battlefield, he was standing (naked still) with his revolver by his side, looking down on a German soldier who had been shot through the eye. We return now. No asterisks are necessary. Perhaps they were not necessary in the first place.

A momentary silence has fallen over the battlefield. His men have seized the enemy trench and so, as usual, the silence indicates that the enemy is regrouping. In a few moments they will return. In this silence, he gazes down at the dead man and various allusions are placed in his mind. He thinks, in fact, about one-eyed monsters and the ill omens that attend them. He shivers and is suddenly acutely aware that he has no clothes. He looks down at his genitals and wonders did he lose his trousers in the course of the fighting. He has seen a man, stripped bare by the force of an explosion, walk away from a near direct hit by a trench mortar. Then he notices that the physical activity of killing has caused a tumescence, not quite a full erection, but a happy state of engorgement such as exists immediately after coitus. He thinks of the woman he has left behind in Bealieu and laughs softly.

The counter-attack must be now or never. The very first round fired will strike him in the chest, just slightly to the left of the heart, but close enough for the bone splinters to rip it open. He spins and falls. The very simplicity of his nakedness, the apparent savagery of it, the barbarian disregard for the niceties of twentieth-century warfare, made him the number one target for German sharpshooters. There is irony in the iron inevitability of it. His revolver and his disregard for his own safety marked him out as an officer. Later he would get a posthumous award for leading the charge and survivors would chuckle over their pints in 1925 and say, 'If the brass only knew,' or, 'They wouldn't have known where to hang it.'

Where to next?

A brother officer, a scholar of the same college at Oxford, arrives to gather his effects. The chaps in the dugout (a major is the highest ranking officer) point them out. 'He was mad,' they say. 'He always slept naked.' Of course, the CO never mentioned that when he wrote to break the bad news. The major says that he hardly thinks it necessary to bother the poor family with the fact that he was ballocks naked when the Hun got him. Nobody laughs. They all loved him.

In a small notebook, in a pocket of the tunic he never put on, the brother officer finds the following words from Horace's fifth ode of the first book: *quis multa gracilis te puer in rosa/per-fusus liquidis urget odoribus/gratto pyrrha sub antro.* And in an often-worked translation underneath: *What slim boy, O Pyrrha, perfumed and drenched in rose-water, have you pressed into service in your privacy now?* From the crossings-out, it is clear that he has already translated and rejected certain words in certain ways: 'smells' for *odoribus,* for example. *Urget* was rendered as 'forcing' at one point and 'ravishing' at another. In particular *perfusus liquidis* was given, in one version, as 'drenched by your juices'. The brother officer understands nothing of the background that we have given his friend, but he understands the pain well enough. And when he finds her letter, his understanding is complete. It is, of course, both unnecessary and unworkmanlike to reproduce the contents of the letter in our story, but we can be certain that they would explain why the officer slept naked, went into battle naked and died naked. And so we return to that initial image.

Why is it that the idea of a man going into battle without underwear or a serge jacket seems so abhorrent?

Dreams

'Alas, poor bollix, I knew him well,' James Deane said. 'That kind of thing. Like, when I started out I hardly knew anyone in there. By the time I was thirty, I knew all the new ones. A corpse is a corpse is a corpse, as they say.' He sucked deeply on his pint and smacked his lips. 'They say you can't take it with you. So, eat drink and be merry, that's what I say.'

Mike Mack sat back against the wall, folded his arms and whistled tunelessly through his teeth. James Deane sucked on his pint again. 'All the same, the Hymac makes all the difference,' he said.

Mike Mack nodded. 'Only for that, hah? You'd wear your shovel out fast enough in this frost. The ground is like a rock.'

'Dead solid.'

'The PP told me a good one,' Mike Mack said, 'about a fella had a lucky escape with a loader. He had one of his kids up on the loader, and he got down to open a gate. The loader was on a bit of a rise, and didn't the kid take it out of gear.'

James Deane sat up, alert, slightly combative.

'He was pinned against the gate pier. He was a lucky man because there was one prong missing from the loader.'

'Jesus Christ,' James Deane said.

'I'm telling you.' Mike Mack shook his head vigorously, once to the left, once to the right. 'One prong went through here.' He made a sweeping gesture as though the prong of a loader came at him and went through his left arm. Another gesture indicated that a second prong had passed harmlessly to his right.

'Lucky enough the second one missed. All that happened was he got bruising and a few crushed ribs. Didn't he get blood poisoning out of it though, hah? That was the worst of it seemingly. E coli. You know where that came from.'

'Kids and machinery.'

'They don't mix.'

'They do not. What'll you have? Same again?'

James Deane signalled to the man behind the bar. The gesture seemed to paralyse him momentarily, his whole face locked halfway between expectation and despair. 'All the same, it's a funny feeling,' he said. 'Burying your own. Kind of savage like. The way it must a been one time.'

'I'd say it is,' Mike Mack said.

'It's funny all right. Some wouldn't do it, but the way I see it, you wouldn't want someone else doing it for you. It's the kind of thing you'd want done for yourself. Your own to do it. Know what I mean?'

Two men came in. They came over to the corner where Mike Mack and James Deane were sitting.

'Oh, the hard men,' James Deane called to them. 'How are you, Lacey?'

Lacey put out his hand and shook James Deane's. 'I'm sorry for your trouble, Jamesy,' he said. The other shook his hand silently.

'Tough old day,' Lacey said.

James Deane shrugged. '*I have done the state some service and they know it.*' Everyone laughed.

'Listen to your man,' Lacey said. 'The guff out of him. Talk about the hard man.'

'That's the way,' Mike Mack said noncommittally.

'Ah Jaze,' Lacey said, 'there's hard and hard in it.'

James Deane looked him up and down. 'They say you wouldn't pay the fifty quid,' he said. 'And your mother's grave buried under a brake of briers. Jesus, you're shit mean, there's no doubt about it.'

Lacey turned red. The second man walked away and stood near the bar watching them in the faded sloping mirror that reflected back their faces and the backs of various bottles.

'Only for the day that's in it,' Lacey said, 'I'd flatten you for that remark.'

'Now now,' Mike Mack said. 'No need for aggro.'

'He buries his own father and here he is quoting poetry? And insulting his neighbours?'

'He's stressed out,' Mike Mack said. 'The whole thing was too much for him.'

'Do me a favour, Lacey,' James Deane said. 'Just fuck off.'

Lacey joined his friend at the bar and they ordered drink. The barman brought two pint glasses on a tray and placed them in front of James Deane and Mike Mack.

'On the house,' he said. 'Boss's orders.'

'Everyone wants to be on the right side of a gravedigger,' James Deane said. The barman chuckled.

'All the same,' Mike Mack said by way of explanation, 'a laugh goes a long way.'

'It goes a long way,' the barman said. 'Give me a shout if there's anything.'

'Will do,' Mike Mack said. 'Cheers, Jamesy.'

James Deane said cheers and they drank.

The barman, now halfway to the bar, turned around and said, 'Why don't you take his place, Jamesy? He was down to the last four for the turkey Thursday night. You could slip into his place. The lads wouldn't mind. A hand of cards'd set you up.

Take your mind off things.'

'You know me and cards,' James Deane said. 'I hate cards.'

'All the same,' Mike Mack said, 'he was going well for the turkey.'

'He'd have won it if his luck was in,' the barman said.

'But his luck was out in earnest,' James Deane said.

'That was desperate all right,' the barman said.

The second man shook his head and said, 'Desperate luck.'

Lacey, rapping the counter sharply with his car keys, looked quizzically at the barman and said, 'Any chance you'd serve us before closing time?'

Mike Mack looked at his watch. The barman picked up two small glasses and shoved them one at a time against the whiskey dispenser. Powers Gold Label. He placed each glass in turn on the counter. Lacey lifted his and drank it off cowboy style.

'And again,' he said and belched gently.

The barman tipped the glass against the dispenser and watched the gold liquid spilling into it.

'You're not driving, Lacey?' he said.

'What's up with you?'

'Only the last time the sergeant was down on me for serving you. And the boss warned me.'

'I know when I had enough.'

'Seemingly some fella sued a pub for giving him a feed of drink and he had an accident on the way home,' Mike Mack said. 'I don't know where I heard that. He sued a hotel and a pub and he won. He was claiming they had no right to be serving him. When he was drunk already.'

'I heard that all right,' the barman said. 'West Cork. The compo culture.'

'Exactly,' Mike Mack said. 'Amazing though. When you come to think about it. Suing a pub for giving you drink.'

'Now you know,' James Deane said to the barman. 'The customer is always right. My arse. Not any more.'

'Anyway,' Lacey said, swinging around and tipping his glass towards James Deane, 'may he rest in peace.'

Everyone murmured agreement and drank. James Deane folded his arms and said 'Amen'. He was thinking of his father stepping along the road with that peculiar gait he had that made him look as if he were avoiding things, stepping lightly between puddles or avoiding patches of dog shit. It got worse after a few pints. He imagined him coming home after playing for the turkey, full of good cheer and boasting about his card-playing skills. Then he saw the oncoming lights and heard the thud as if he had been there himself. His father had been blown on to the windscreen, the guards said, judging by the fragments of glass and the lacerations. It shouldn't be hard to track down a car with that much damage.

He shuddered.

'All right, Jamesy?' Mike Mack asked.

'I was thinking about my father,' James Deane said.

'God rest him,' Mike Mack added.

'Any news of the car?' the barman called.

James Deane shook his head. 'The sergeant says he has a good idea all right,' he said.

'Fuck the sergeant,' Lacey said. 'If he got off his fat arse and got out of the squad car every couple of weeks, he might do something. If he concentrated on catching hit-and-runs instead of honest citizens going home with a few scoops on board.'

'That's the whole point, isn't it?' James Deane said. 'It's the same thing.'

Lacey glared at him.

'She'll kill me,' Mike Mack said, looking at his watch again. 'I'm late already. The dinner'll be frazzled.'

'At least you'll have the pleasure of being buried by your own Hymac,' James Deane said.

Mike Mack got up to go, seemed to think better of it, said, 'Are you all right so, Jamesy?' Then, when Jamesy shook his fist at him in mock anger, went after all, bracing himself when the opened door admitted a wintry daylight. 'Good luck, men,' he called and the door slammed.

Much later, stumbling out of the friendly babble, the day now gone and not enough of the night, James Deane wondered how he would face the road home past the spot where his father died. How he would find the house cold and silent. That morning, before the funeral, he had stood in front of the hall stand straightening his tie and had seen in the mirror, hanging on a nail behind the door, the huge scarf he had bought his father last Christmas to keep the cold out of his weak throat. He had stepped out of the reflection, swallowing something hard that would not go down.

And when the PP asked him if he would prefer not to dig the grave, that Mike Mack said he could do the job on his own with the Hymac, he had said that it was the least he could do. He would dig deep, as deep as he could go with his mother already in there, and he would square it neat, and he would make sure Mike Mack didn't make shit of it with the claw which he was likely to. Just to break the cold surface, the first foot of ground that would be as hard as concrete; after that it would be the shovel.

In a way, he thought, it was like putting his father to bed. He would stretch him out and pull his shoes off and shuffle the blankets out from under him. 'Goodnight now, Dad,' he used to say. He always whispered it, like it was a child and not his father. And all night he would be disturbed by the old man's dreams that came to him in drink, filling the next room and the draughty landing and coming in like a draught under his own door. The sound of his mother dying over and over each night in the old man's head. And in the morning the old man would wonder how he got to bed. 'Jesus, Jamesy,' he'd say, 'I must have been very bad last night.' And James would say, 'You were rotten out, Dad. I had to put you to bed again.' 'I had terrible dreams,' the old man used to say. 'Desperate dreams.'

From the Hughes Banana

There was something suspicious in the light (beige sunlight on beige walls), something unrealistically later about the day. Dolman checked his watch. It was still eleven thirty a.m. It had to be more than a minute since he looked at it last. He looked around him at the corridor he was in. Opaque windows glowed with the suggestion of an outside world, but the light was that unpleasant neutral colour. He thought of it as unrealistic, like the lighting in a bad movie. The linoleum was beige, too, and the walls were beige. A moving walkway carried people by at speed, some towing suitcases on wheels. He could hear the wheels squeaking. An electronic sign said BAGGAGE ←. He guessed he was in an airport. He checked his watch again. Eleven thirty-one.

So nothing was stuck.

The date was the fifteenth. A Wednesday. He searched his pockets and found his wallet.

There was an airline ticket.

LAX.

Los Angeles Airport, 1 World Way, Los Angeles.

But what was he doing here?

Hughes Air had delivered him in its big yellow aeroplane, the Hughes Banana: Spokane, Washington; Yakima; Seattle; Portland, Oregon; Salem; Eugene; Medford, Oregon; Las Vegas; and LAX – the names were magical, like some kind of old Indian incantation, or the lists of railway stations conductors used to call just as the train was leaving – '*All aboard for . . .*' –

full of mystery and becoming. Now he was at the end of the line. LAX.

But was he here to address three hundred people on the politics of inter-office rivalry, or was he going to have to sit and listen to someone else delivering it? Or was he interviewing MBA graduates? Or was he hiring or firing someone from the LA office?

Or maybe he was on vacation.

Could it be that at last he had taken a break?

Unlikely. He was finding it increasingly hard to get away. Work, weirdly fulfilling more and more of his needs, demanding less and less of his brain, had digested so much of his waking life, and some of his sleeping, too. Anyway, LA was especially unlikely. If Dolman ever took a vacation, it would be to somewhere out in the boondocks, hillbilly country, where the good old boys never washed their hands coming out of the bathroom, where they served pitchers of beer and tenderloin pork sandwiches, and the talk going round was of the price of wheat and the Little League. He would pick up a couple of pounds of kielbasa sausages, head for a cabin in the woods with a trout stream out back. He'd steam the sausages in beer, then brown them in butter in the pan the way his mother used to. He could almost smell it now.

Just a cabin in the woods out in the boondocks in good-old-boy country.

A place where nobody bought insurance.

Definitely never LA.

He took out his monthly organiser. He looked at it for a moment with some surprise, then he checked Wednesday 15. *It all comes together in the end*, he thought, *and nobody is ever really lost.*

A seminar on corporate sponsorship. He wasn't flying back

until Saturday. He would be a listener this time, although he could already predict what would be said. The big question: now that government is cutting back on the different ways you can get your snout in the trough, how can *we* (corporations are always personal pronouns) keep giving *our*selves parties and still write it off for corporation tax. (The answer: hire a public relations firm and call it advertising. It's still a golf classic for *our* clients and *our*selves, but now it's corporate sponsorship and advertising. Everybody knew it, but the seminar was also tax deductible in several interesting ways.)

So he was in LA for three days.

Next question: where was he staying?

He thought about the hotels he knew, rolled their names around his head hoping that one of them would make a sound: St Bonaventure, Excelsior, Sheraton, Crown Plaza, Hyatt, even Motel 6. For a minute he thought that old 6 was going to ring his bell, but in the end it didn't, so he rang his office manager.

'Tony? I'm in LA? I can't remember where I'm staying. Did you book me in the Excelsior?'

'Jim? I'll just check that one.' Long silence. 'It was the Crown Plaza. You wanted that, remember? Same place as last time. Remember?'

Dolman said that it had slipped his mind. His speech, he noticed, was a little thick, as though he had been drinking. Tony obviously thought so. There was a faint tone of subdued expectation coming down the ether. *The boss hit the sauce on the plane. By the time he got to LA he couldn't remember where he was staying . . .*

'Have a good one.'

'You too.'

Never out of touch with a cellular phone, he thought. *Never out of touch.*

A brochure landed on his desk recently. It showed a worried man, hand splayed across his face, the single visible eye staring upwards, slightly moist. *You're representing your company in a crowd of unfamiliar faces*, the leaflet screamed. What do you do? The solution was a one-day seminar on working the crowd. How to remember faces. How to work a business or social event. How to gain critical information and identify potential customers quickly. How to maximise your use of time at events and functions such as exhibitions, meetings, launches and lunches. How not to come on strong and yet leave a positive impression and a desire to follow up. *Think opportunity*, the leaflet insisted. *Think network. Think impact. Think impression. Network with confidence.*

Dolman looked around and realised that he was in a crowd of unfamiliar faces, and yet he knew everyone.

Samsonite was still the luggage of choice for the busy executive. Black or grey Samsonites went round the carousel, wobbling purposefully like Chaplins. It struck Dolman that a god somewhere out in the galaxies, the boondocks of the universe, might actually enjoy the behaviour of a hundred thousand carousels swirling and spitting cases. He might see a kaleidoscope – here and in Singapore and Heathrow and Charles de Gaulle and JFK and all the other thousands of carousels – always busy, always carrying the same Samsonite bags, sucking them in and spitting them out all purpose and fuss.

It might amuse the god to switch the carousels.

Now Dolman and the guy next door who, according to his laptop case, worked for Xerox, and the guy beyond that whose face he recognised from a previous flight: each would see his case come out of the flux, each would pick it up and carry it to his version of the Crown Plaza, and in a room exactly like any other room in any other hotel, he would open it up to remove the washbag – to take a shower, to take his Prozac, to retrieve the picture of the kids – and find, for example, that he was a traveller in ladies underwear of the most expensive kind, or that the case was full of used hundred-dollar bills.

What would they do?

They would fish in their pockets for their airline ticket, their wallet, their monthly organiser and start putting the clues together.

'Excuse me asking this,' Dolman said. He coughed artificially. It was an apology and accepted as such. He stared at the floor for a moment. His shoes, he noticed, were scuffed around the toes. It never did happen when he was married. No amount of attention to his own appearance made up for the absence of that critical eye. And his hair, he had noticed recently, was flecked grey. He had been taken by surprise once again, but a partner would have drawn his attention to the very first strand. The slight paunch was a troubling presence, too. He needed exercise.

They were queuing at the information desk, fifth or sixth in line, Xerox and Dolman, waiting to see what their fate would be. They had settled into an apparently casual conversation. As it happened, they had both grown up in Seattle, Washington. They both remembered the same TV sketch about lost luggage but hadn't yet been able to figure out which show it was from. They had both attended the University of Washington, though in different years.

'Excuse me asking this. I'm guessing you fly a lot, same as me. Ever wake up in a hotel room and not know where you were?'

He was worried. He was aware of something going on in his body – in his head most probably. He was sweating. He could taste it on his lips. He felt as if his whole body was quivering slightly, nothing an outsider would notice, but inside, where the nerve endings connected with the surface, substance was wavering, fluctuating, liquefying. He felt as if his entire self was turning quietly into perspiration.

'It happens to me a lot lately,' he said. 'I wake up in a room and I've just had a nightmare. I'm lost. I wake up and I'm still lost, but now I'm definitely awake. So I sit up, determined to hit this thing on the head right away. I look around for evidence. I've got a travelling clock. There's a bunch of papers on the table. I'm trying to think where this room should be. There are pictures on the walls, but they could be from anywhere. In fact, I recognise some of them from other places. You see the same views in airports, offices, magazines. Dime-a-dozen art: sunsets, people fly-fishing, horses, sailboats. So I turn on all the lights, but there's nothing in the room to give me a clue. I could be anywhere.'

Xerox was interested now, caught up in the drama of Dolman's bewilderment. He was angular, long-faced, pale-eyed. He was tilted slightly away so that he appeared to be looking at Dolman across the bridge of his nose.

'So what do you do?'

'Well, you can't call the desk and say: where the hell am I?'

Xerox nodded. He understood that one.

'They'll send the men from the funny farm. So, what do I do? I get my clothes. Sometimes there's an airline ticket or a taxi receipt, a restaurant check.'

Xerox smiles. This makes sense. It's the way to go.

'But then I start to wonder if that restaurant was in this city. Maybe it's an old receipt and I'm someplace else now. I get my watch and press the date button. Oh, so it's the twelfth. The check is for the tenth. It doesn't tell me anything. Do I have a monthly organiser? I fish in my coat pocket.'

Xerox was nodding his head enthusiastically now, short jabbing eager nods.

'I'm flying three, four times a week now.'

Xerox said, 'There's always something. I know it.'

'They're all sort of smoothing out. Blending.'

'So. In the bedroom? You were lost, remember.'

Dolman comes back slowly from the contemplation of a universe that was slowly smoothing out, losing its distinctness. 'I find the organiser. I relax. Now I know where I am.'

'Exactly,' Xerox says. 'It's simple. As long as the organiser is up to date.'

'You cross-check, of course.'

'Of course.'

'There's the date on the watch. That's reliable. Good old quartz. Then there's the trail of receipts. Dates in the organiser. It all pans out in the end. You go back to sleep. Everything is OK.'

'Exactly.'

'So,' Dolman said, 'how about you?'

Xerox stepped back a little, a subtle change in the angles. Now the tilt puts a prominent cheekbone in the way. The glance is sideways. 'No, I don't get that. I heard about it, but it never happens to me. I met a guy from Metropolitan Life that got it. One weird guy.'

'I work for the Met.'

Xerox took another half-step back. 'Have we met before?'

'I don't think so.'

'Are you based in Seattle?'

'Eugene, Oregon.'

Silence. They stared combatively at each other for a moment, then looked away.

'Jeez, insurance. How do you do it?'

Dolman was piqued. 'What do you do? Sell photocopiers?'

The clerk behind the sign that said Information said, 'Next, please.'

'I have never been a salesman.'

'Well, let me tell you, don't speak too soon. Wait and see what the gods have planned to screw up *your* day.'

Xerox swivelled on his heel and pressed as close to the desk as he could get. Dolman could hear him say that it was the second time his baggage had been lost. This time they would hear from his lawyers. He had had it up to here. He would be recommending to his company that they fly United or Northwest Orient in future, anything but the frapping Hughes Banana. 'Last time, the bag came back torn and with some items missing. It was stamped Fiumicino, that's Italy, for Christ's sake. They sent it halfway round the world. What kind of a damn airline was this anyway?'

'I just missed my connection,' Xerox said. 'I think.'

'I'm supposed to be at the Crown Plaza. Seminar on sponsorship.'

'We use the Sheraton.'

'The San Francisco Sheraton is good.'

'Do you really think they're going to find our luggage?'

Dolman shrugged. 'I'm losing it,' he said.

'Me too. This is my second time in LAX. Last time they lost it they sent it to Italy, for God sakes.'

'All these places are the same.'

'Not Italy. You ever been to Italy? Jesus Christ! I was there with my ex in '85 or '86. It's different over there.'

The carousel was suddenly moving again. A single yellow suitcase came through the gate and moved slowly in front of their seat. Their eyes followed it round speculatively.

Xerox had his laptop between his knees.

The yellow suitcase was not Samsonite.

'Sort of lapses. Things going missing.'

'The way they drive. Jeez. I tell you something: ever go to Italy, don't hire a car. Take the frapping train.'

'Sometimes I wonder if I'm getting the right stuff. Like, everything drops out for a few minutes, and when I come back, maybe, just maybe –' Dolman raised his eyebrows meaningfully '– maybe when it comes back I have the wrong stuff, but I don't know it's different because I can't make the connections. Or maybe I'm coming back to the wrong place.'

'You think: I like eating Italian, I go to the trattorias downtown, I should like Italy. Hey, at business school I was a fan of Fellini even. Can you believe that? I was the only guy in business school with a soul.'

'Since my wife walked out on me I keep getting it. It's like there's no one fixed point.'

'My ex walked away with the house, the car, the dog, *and* the frapping alimony.' Xerox laughed. 'She could've had the dog without any proceedings.'

The suitcase had disappeared temporarily. Now it came through the plastic curtain and set off on its circular route once again. It wobbled comically at the bends.

'I like dogs.'

'Well, I don't see you walking one right now.'

What if that suitcase was a bomb? *I mean, a yellow suitcase? It doesn't happen. In twenty years I never saw a yellow suitcase that somebody forgot.*

'At least she couldn't take the kids because we never had any.'

Dolman stood up. 'You know what I think? I think I don't *have* luggage.'

Xerox stared at him. 'Sure you have. Everybody has luggage.'

Dolman held his hands out, palms out. They did not quiver. 'You see any luggage?'

'They *said* they lost it. That's what they said.'

'That's what they *said*. They'll say anything to get you off their case.'

Now Xerox was standing, too. He hoisted his laptop by its shoulder strap and, in one smooth, practised movement, looped it over his right shoulder. That eagerness was back. His head was jabbing again, the same short stabs of his jaw. 'So, what're you going to do?'

'I'm going to check in at the Plaza and wait.'

'Wait?'

'Wait. See what gives. Let the bastards come to me.'

'I see it. It's a strategy.' Xerox looked boyish almost. Dolman could see the college student in him all of a sudden, the fraternity kid childishly eager to thumb his nose at the faculty, good for a prank, a Greek Week wheeze.

'I'm in the Plaza. I know where I am. *They* want *me.*'

'Exactly.'

'They can come and get me.'

A man in a turban picked up the yellow suitcase and dropped it onto its wheels. He extended a collapsing handle and began to walk towards the arrivals lounge.

'Don't take any calls,' Xerox said. 'Make them face you, one on one.'

'One on one.' They smiled at each other.

'I wish I could go with you,' Xerox said, 'but I have to make this connection . . .'

'I'll lie low. See who they send.'

'That way you know who's out there.'

'What you think, how long do I have?'

'Three, four days. The organiser'll tell you. When you

don't get back, they'll start to think about it. They'll call the hotel.'

'They'll try to reel me in.'

The intercom bing-bonged. 'Mr James Dolman, Mr James Dolman, please come to the information desk. Mr James Dolman.'

Xerox shifted his angles again, head inclined so that the information desk was in his sights. 'That's your case they're calling. They found it.'

'I don't see it.'

'They have it out back, maybe.'

'I'm out of here,' Dolman said. 'If I don't stop now, I'm finished.'

'Good luck.' They clasped hands and smiled momentarily. This was a good one, this was the way to go, to get out while there was still time.

Dolman turned to face the exit. 'Have one on me,' Xerox called, 'when you're out.'

The PA boomed again, and Dolman heard himself named. He remembered that his travel alarm was in his suitcase. And the book he was reading: *Coping with Stress: How to Be Successful and Survive.* He had picked it up at a seminar a month ago. He read so slowly now, always asleep before the page turned, always backtracking to find what he had missed. There was some useful stuff in that book.

'You really think they have my case?' He glanced back over his shoulder and saw that angled head, the eyes peering upwards now.

Xerox shook his head and looked away. He was calculating again, instantly noncommittal, vigilant. 'That depends,' he said. 'What kind of a case was it?'

Nero Was an Angler

1

At first she thought he just looked pale in the beautiful crowd, but when she passed a second time she noticed that he was not so much pale as iron-grey. When he called, it was the accent she noticed first, surprised that she could still detect the sound of home. Then she realised he was calling her. It was the faintest signal in the static babble that is an Italian beach.

'You're Irish,' he said when she came closer.

'And you?' she said. He smiled slightly. He seemed out of breath, as though the effort of calling had been too much.

'Are you all right?'

He motioned to the empty deckchair beside him and said, 'Please.'

It was a cordial, magical gesture. She thought of it at once as ambassadorial, something from her grandparents' time, Victorian or even older. It reminded her of the way certain men opened a door or rose from a chair in a seamless almost balletic movement in which they passed from one state of being to another without appearing to make a transition. Its fluidity astonished her, and yet it was pregnant with all kinds of courtesy, regard and perhaps even affection.

She sat down.

She could hear his laboured breathing clearly now. Again she asked, 'Are you all right?'

'Very kind of you,' he said. 'Isn't this lovely?'

He indicated the flat dark waters of the lake, the blue sky, the crowds.

'Very unusual for this time of year.'

'Did you come down by the bus? It's a long way from the town down here. It's a volcano crater, you know?'

'Yes, I took the bus.'

'The water is wonderful. So bright.'

'Nero was an angler in the lake of darkness,' he said.

A party of chattering boys made conversation temporarily impossible. Then a boy arrived with a bus conductor's satchel to collect the money for the chair. When she turned to look at him again, he was asleep.

She guessed he was in his seventies, reasonably well-off, a tourist rather than a resident. He looked settled and ordinary in his sleep. She looked for his left hand and saw no ring, not even the tell-tale polished band of skin. Still, she felt comfortable and somehow at home with him, as if she were sitting with her own father, as if that would be possible. She was tired, having walked the town all morning, having eaten well. She pulled the brim of her hat down, folded her hands on her stomach and went to sleep as easily as a child.

The sound of the boy closing deckchairs awakened her. The beach was emptying. The sun was low over the hill, and the last couple were being handed ashore from the rowing boat. A train was moving through the trees on the hill at her back. She recognised the sound almost before she was awake.

The man beside her was no longer breathing. She did not need to touch him to know that he was dead.

She stood up and pointed at the boy. '*Aiutami,*' she called, '*Quest'uome è morto. Parla Inglese?*'

The boy nodded.

'We must find a doctor,' she said. '*Un medico.*'

And then she thought that perhaps they should also find a priest. And a policeman.

'I will get the manager,' the boy said. He was unperturbed. Perhaps people died all the time on the beach at Castelgandalfo. Pilgrims who made one last-ditch effort to see the pope. Perhaps it was a commonplace. She could even imagine that some company somewhere organised tours for the dying, for the soon-to-be inactive retired. She began to cry.

2

He stood at the end of the queue with the extension handle of his suitcase resting against his thigh. The Englishwoman who earlier had been extolling the virtues of wheeled cases was fanning herself with a brochure advertising one of the knick-knack shops on the square. He remembered that one whole shelf had been lined with statuettes of popes. To judge by the space allotted to each, John XXIII was still the most popular, followed by the present incumbent. The owner watched them carefully. Did pilgrims often steal popes? he wondered. His father would have been interested to know. He wished he could speak Italian. He would have liked to raise the matter with her. Did she think she suffered more or less theft as a result of having her business next door to the summer residence? Which nationality was the worst? The Irish? The Italians? The Poles? And then: could it be that piety and covetousness were linked? Each virtue to its vice?

Now the tour guide was talking. Most of the travellers were English, but there were four Germans and a French couple and himself, the sole Irish representative. English Roman Catholics he judged to be more devout than their Irish counterparts, although his experience of either was limited.

'And what brings you here?' he had asked at a breakfast table in Rome. He had been trying to make conversation on their first morning.

How many days ago was that? Something had gone wrong with his body. Walking down the steps from the aeroplane into the heat of Ciampino he had felt it, a wobble in time or space. He felt half-in and half-out of everything, as though one side of his body – the right-hand side – were not involved. He was clumsy. He had knocked glasses off a table. He had crashed into an oncoming Englishwoman so hard that he had knocked her glasses off. And then he did not hear everything, and sometimes even found that when he spoke no sound issued. But on this occasion he had spoken clearly enough.

'What brings me here? I came to pray where Peter prayed,' the woman had replied to his question. She stated it as if it were the obvious answer. As if a million people came to Rome every day for only that purpose.

'*I* came because it was cheap,' he said. 'A last-minute offer.'

In fact, he had been surprised to discover where exactly the tour was going. David had always looked after details.

Now that the queue was complete and everyone had left the shelter and comfort of the hotel, it turned out that the bus had some 'technical difficulties'. The guide repeated the euphemism in the three languages of the tour, and when she had finished, a man at the front said, 'It's bloody broken down, hasn't it?'

'It's the Italians,' the woman with the fan said to him. 'They've always been inefficient. At least Mussolini made the trains run on time.'

He turned around and walked away. The rumble of his case followed him. *Give them an hour*, he thought. And then he began to think about what would happen if he didn't show up. Would they go without him? Would they set the police after him? He had seen them in their immaculate striped uniforms, with their white holsters. They were almost invariably in the company of beautiful women. He envied them their youth and their beauty. He had always loved physical perfection first. He had envied David his big dark eyes and his mass of gleaming hair. He would like to be at the start again, with possibility before him, naivety and conviction his only weapons.

3

She kept having to ask the policeman to slow down. '*Piano, piano,*' she said. '*Più lentamente, per favore.*' Each time he would slow for a sentence and then gradually increase speed. He could not understand how it was that she came to be sitting beside this old dying man when she did not know him, not even his name. It was truly astonishing. And this about Nero. Did it refer to the emperor Nero? Did the old man mean that Nero came to Castelgandalfo to fish?

Why *did* she sit down? She supposed it was because he was Irish, because he was gentle and reminded her of her father. Because he asked. Now she wondered why she had not tried to engage him in conversation, but she recalled her relief at being able to take the weight off her feet, at hearing the soft accent, at being stationary for once. She had been travelling for such a long time.

Now she was going to have to stay, at least until they had completed their enquiries and identified the man. She would have to find a hotel, easy today at least because it was a Monday. She would need to find work if it was more than a few days. She had, she supposed, if she were careful, a week at most. Perhaps she should count on staying that long and bargain a better rate. The policeman warned her not to leave the town and to let him know as soon as she had a place to stay. He gave her a little printed card with his name. Crescenzo di Fiore. It sounded more like an operatic event. She pronounced it and he smiled. He said, in English, 'Everybody thinks it is funny. It is because I am Neapolitan. The name.'

He touched the card with the tip of his index finger. He was looking directly at her.

'From Naples?' she said.

'Where one finds Neapolitans,' he replied.

She walked up the hill. It was cooler now. Boys and girls passed on their scooters, sometimes two or three abreast, shaking hands, talking, waving, swerving to avoid oncoming cars. When she reached the streets, the same people seemed to be going by, calling out to friends in bars and doorways. All of Italy seemed to be taking the unseasonably warm October air. She walked up onto the belvedere and looked down the steep slope, several hundred metres, to the beach. Now the lake was a pool of darkness. The more she looked at it, the more it seemed like she was staring into nothing. There were no lights, no reflections except at the very far edge, no reference points with which to judge distance. She might have been looking outwards into the galaxy, losing herself in the cold lightlessness of the past.

She must find a hotel.

4

He hired a punt and arranged with the young woman who took the cash that he should leave his suitcase with her. A young man helped him in, explaining in carefully rehearsed English that he must be back in one hour, one hour. The young man caught his wrist and tapped the face of his watch. 'One hour? Understood?'

He pulled out onto the lake, surprised to find that the old skills were still there. He loosened his tie and then took it off altogether. Then he took his jacket off and made a cushion of it. He sensed there was a current that moved him counter-clockwise around the edge of the lake, and he decided to go with it, even though he knew he would pay for his laziness on the way back. The woods rose directly up from the shore now and culminated in the walls of the old town. On top of everything was the bastion of the castle and the pope's residence.

Yesterday he had surprised everybody by opting not to take the tour. He could not explain to them that he had seen enough of the papacy in the entrance to the Sistine Chapel, thousands of years of rapacity represented by ornate crucifixes, pieces of ancient altar ware, maps and globes and clocks and tapestries, the whole culminating in a foolish glass swan, life size or larger, donated by the faithful of America. His father had been right.

But he was looking forward to the chapel.

First he looked behind the altar at the *Last Judgement*. He had been studying the guidebook and knew what he was looking for – Michelangelo's self-portrait in the hollow skin of St Bartholomew who was flayed alive. The saint, risen whole for judgment day, holds his own hide as casually as a coat, and the artist's face gazes out of it. Self-portrait of a hollow man. Boundless despair on the *dies iræ*. But when he found it, he was dismayed. The distortion was unbearable. He looked into Michelangelo's empty sockets and saw the ghosts of eyes that should have been immortal.

When, in time, he made his way down the steps and looked around him, he was surprised to find himself surrounded by whispering, tilted people, the crowd he came in with it seemed, still here, anxious to see as much as possible of the ceiling because it had taken so long to paint. As though it were a famous feat of athletics, the gold medal for painting and endurance.

He liked them. He believed he would like to have their capacity for trust. He had stood with them in Rome and stared at the ceiling until his neck ached, but yesterday he had baulked in the little square in Castelgandalfo. He had stopped at the door with the keys of Peter above it, feeling that he could not bear to pretend any more.

'No, thank you,' he said to the Englishwoman who was urging him. 'I'm a little tired. I think I might sit in that café there.'

She had taken to him, he felt sure. He had seen her chuckling that first morning at the breakfast table when he had told her friend that he came because the flight was a bargain, and later she had taken him aside and said, 'Well done, you! She *is* a pompous ass at times, even if she is my friend.' They were travelling together but he detected some friction between them.

'I'm not feeling myself,' he said. 'I'm out of sorts. I'd only hold you all back. Go ahead without me. I'll still be here when you get back.'

The guide had been solicitous. 'Are you sure you'll be all right?'

But impatient also. She kept looking past him to the man at the door.

Now, while he pulled slowly out onto the eye of the lake, she would be counting heads in the bus. She would panic. Or perhaps they were trained for such eventualities and some system would go into action.

He looked down into the water and was defeated by it. How deep? A thousand feet? These old craters went down and down. Someone had told him once that the depth around the Greek islands was more than three thousand feet. If he jumped in now, he would sink – how far? At some point, perhaps, the density of the water would prevent him from going further. Was that possible? He would float halfway between utter darkness and the bright surface. But in the end, the lake would throw him back.

The lake of darkness, he thought. *Nero was an angler in the lake of darkness.* Where did that come from? Was it a poem? It sounded like the beginning of some old ballad. If he reached back now, he could probably find an air to fit it. He began to hum as he rowed. He passed the children at play on the little beaches that had private pathways leading down to them. He passed the boat-houses with their immaculate mahogany slipper-boats. He passed little olive groves with their ancient twisted human forms. One last house, washed in faded yellow, glowed against the gloom of the trees. And away over the eastern rim, in a cobalt blue sky, a million starlings wheeled in a huge column on an updraft, like fish in a tropical shoal, marvellous and ordinary.

5

The Hotel Belvedere had two rooms available – the one facing the lake was dearer but she took it just the same, knowing that it was foolish. When she opened the window to look down, there were lights moving on the surface and the illusion of infinity was gone. The room was simple but clean. The furniture was old, the bathroom tiles were cracked in places, the mirror was missing some silvering. She took her clothes off and stood in the shower. First the cool was good, then when she had enough of that the hot started to come through and she felt her skin tingle. She turned slowly in the stream. She had not had a man in months. From what she had seen of Castelgandalfo, she was not likely to get lucky tonight.

She thought about the man who had died by the lake. It occurred to her that perhaps he knew he was dying when he called her. But why did he choose her? She was not the youngest or most beautiful woman. The Italian girls stunned her some-times – the perfect shape, the face, the hair. No other nation in Europe compared, she thought, not even the French of Paris.

She had been travelling Europe for seven years now, spoke French, German, Spanish and Italian well – French best, perhaps – and could get by in other languages. She had lived by teaching English, by waitressing, by picking fruit for four awful weeks, even by giving guided tours. She saved for six months, working diligently, spending nothing, and then moved on, spending as she went, until everything ran out and she had to start again. For eight months she had lived in a flat near the Rue Mouff as the mistress of a French lawyer, but his insistent questions had worn her down, and one evening, after he went home, she had walked out and caught the night train south. She had felt, she once told him, like a *client,* as though he were trying to get to the bottom of her the better to defend her. But she did not need, or want, to be defended.

The man who died, on the other hand, seemed to her to be the stay-at-home type, rooted somewhere to a family and friends, some small community where he absolutely belonged. His trousers were tight and turned up at the ends. His shirt was cotton with a very faint blue check. He wore leather shoes and they had leather soles. She could almost hear his footfall in a house somewhere in Ireland, the distinct flap of the leather going down, a sharp strong sound. He would have been a strong man, a pillar of strength once.

She dressed and went out. She found a restaurant and was shown to a table by a window. The lake was there again. She went home directly after her meal and closed the shutters. At least in the morning the sun would be shining.

6

Something was happening, he knew. There were strange effects in the light. Certain things seemed whiter than they should be. He could hear a noise in his head like a circulation pump gulping air and water. His arms were tired. He looked at his watch, but he could not remember what time he had started out. He tried to remember when the bus was due to depart. He thought it was eleven o'clock, but that was almost three hours ago.

He shipped the oars and took his jacket out from under him and put it over his head. The shade was good, but very soon the heat was too much. He held it up over his head like a parasol until his arms got tired. He tried to scoop water up, but it dribbled out of his hand.

It struck him suddenly that none of this was happening. There was something preposterous and dreamlike about it. Irrational was the word that suggested itself. Irrational like a dream. This being in Italy, on a pilgrimage, being alone.

And if that were the case, there would be no consequences. One morning he would wake up, and everything would be as it was when he fell asleep except that the clock had moved on. If he relinquished any attempt to influence events, he would be carried along to whatever resolution awaited, if resolution were to be part of the dream, or at least carried through the sequence or series of events or phenomena or whatever they might be called until the time came to wake. He laughed at the thought. He could resist the absurdity by not resisting. What was the phrase he heard? Go with the flow.

And now, almost immediately, proof presented itself. A man in a fibreglass boat with an outboard motor was chugging towards him and holding up the end of a rope. In a moment he was alongside and fastening the rope to an eye in the bow of the little punt. They did not speak until the knot was tied. Then the man looked at him and said, 'OK? Hold tight, understood? Hold tight?' And he recognised him as the young man who had cast him off earlier in the day. Who had tapped his wristwatch.

He tapped him on the leg now and looked into his face. '*Va bene?* OK?'

'Yes. I'm OK. OK.'

'OK.'

He pushed the two boats apart and throttled up slowly. The rope gradually took up the slack and they began to move back towards the beach. The pace was slow. The outboard motor had 2.5 on the side. That, he assumed, was the horsepower. It reminded him of the funeral. His was the first car after the hearse; he had insisted on that, on his rights, and he had felt, at the time, like someone in a disabled car being towed very cautiously and hesitantly to the scrapyard. Ahead of him, the black coffin gleamed in the steely autumn sunlight. *I'm alone now*, he had thought, and the same desolation had come over him in various ways and at various times every day since then, as often as he had thought of David. In the rear-view mirror, he could see the disapproving family, the nephew driving, and behind that perhaps ten cars. All the little skullcaps bobbed in the crowd, and further back, among the young, baseball caps. He supposed that if David had been a woman, no one would have turned up. The line lies on the female side. The graveyard was on a hillside that looked down at the river. Mist and smoke from fires combined to make everything uncertain. He felt like a stranger, an onlooker at the curious ritual.

7

The tiny breakfast room was cold and shabby, the atmosphere warmed only by the smell of coffee. She ordered a milky bowl and cradled it in both hands, ignoring the plain bread and little plastic pots of butter and preserve. The same woman who had given her the key last night now operated the coffee machine. On the subject of whether she had slept well, she had lied for simplicity's sake. In fact, she had awoken after two or three dreamy hours and found it difficult to get back to sleep. For a time she had sat with the shutter open. Then, about four o'clock, she closed the window, turned on the light and wrote a letter home. She wrote slowly and twice tore away the sheet. Then, this morning, she had asked at the desk for an envelope. Once the coffee had warmed her and cleared her head, she addressed the envelope to her mother and folded the pages inside.

A man came in and spoke to the woman, who indicated her table, the only one occupied in the breakfast room, as it happened. The man turned and looked at her, and she saw that it was the policeman. He said something to the woman and then came and asked if she'd mind if he sat down.

'How did you know I was here?'

He smiled. 'The telephone,' he said. 'I telephoned.'

She saw him reading the address on the envelope upside down and wondered if insatiable curiosity was an entry requirement in all police forces. The belief that no item of information, no matter how small, should be allowed to go to waste.

He asked her if she had slept well and then remarked that the weather was beautiful again today. Did she know that the pope was here? One could tell because the papal flag was flying over the residence. It was most strange at this time of year. People said he would die at Castelgandalfo, as Paul did. Perhaps it was happening at the very moment. If so, it would be a serious headache for the police. The traffic alone would be horrible.

The woman arrived with a glass of water and a coffee in a tiny blue cup. He drank half the water and then half the coffee. Then he sipped the water for a few moments in silence before finishing the coffee.

Would she mind answering one more question?

She said she would be as helpful as she could be, but he must understand that she did not know the man. That she had spoken only a few words to him and really all that she remembered was what he said about Nero.

The policeman dismissed her reservation with a wave of his hand. 'It is nothing,' he said. 'Poetry.' He believed it was a poem by William Shakespeare, the English poet and dramatist.

It was clear to her that he, or someone else, had checked it out, that the policeman had read the actual reference. A methodical man, then.

'You think he was Irish?'

'Yes.'

'It was the Irish dialect perhaps?'

She had often explained to Europeans that Irish was a language, not a dialect. She did not feel up to it this morning.

'No. It was the pronunciation. He pronounced the words as an Irish person would. I knew it immediately. As you would recognise an Italian.'

'You're certain then?'

'Yes. I would say he was a retired teacher, because of the way he dressed. Very conservative, you understand? Even a priest. Why not? A priest on a pilgrimage? Or a civil servant maybe. In Ireland civil servants do not dress fashionably.'

He drank half of what was left in the water glass. He did not have a wedding ring. She smiled at him.

'It is possible,' he said. 'In fact we have not been able to find his luggage. One missing person has been reported by an English tour group. They will fax his booking details to us later in the day, and of course we will check with the airline. It is only a matter of time: airlines are much more careful now. But at present, all we know is that he joined the group at the same time as everyone else in London.'

'There's nothing unusual in that.'

The policeman shrugged. It was an affirmative shrug. Now he thanked her and rose to go. She almost expected him to turn at the door and say, 'One last question.' But instead he waved and called, '*Ci vediamo.*' We'll meet again. We'll see each other again. It was the kind of thing friends said. See you later.

8

The young man helped him out of the boat. This habit of looking directly into the face but not into the eyes – what was he looking for? The pontoon against which they tied was unsteady, and the glare from the water made it worse. The young man took his arm and led him to the sand.

'I'll be all right,' he said. 'I'm all right. I'm going to take a walk. I've been sitting too long.'

The young man said something in Italian and pointed at the sky. 'The sun,' he said. 'OK?'

'I'm OK,' the man said. 'Thank you.'

'*Prego.*'

As he walked away, he had the impression that the young man was still watching him, waiting for him to turn round so he could study his face again. *Maybe he wants to remember me*, the man thought, *in case I stole something from the boat. These amusement people are always suspicious.*

The pump-sound in his head had receded, to be replaced by the drone of the outboard, which, detached now from the actual engine, seemed to have a life of its own, complete with the sputtering irregularity that overtook it whenever the young man moved in his seat. His arms felt like lead. How long since he had pulled a boat?

A man indicated a selection of deckchairs. He chose one that had an umbrella, paid his money and sat gratefully into the shade. Within the circle, in the well-defined penumbra, the air was actually cool. It surprised him. A window blinked on the far shore. If he moved his head slightly, it didn't look at him.

He recalled his father bringing the boat home after dark, following the beacon in. When a lighthouse closes for ever, they say the light is extinguished. Up and down the coast, the small marks, sensible, unmoving, the first sign of home. The entrance is an easy one, but the light helps. There are the islands, so close to shore they are indistinguishable. High Island on the port hand, not so high as solitary. And foul grounds inside.

Glide past the point, keeping to the far shore where the water runs deep – the shoal is always on the inside curve. You will see the lights of the village, our house on the hill. If it is evensong, the church windows will stand up straight among the yews, higher than any of us. The smell of tea will drift out over the water: rashers and sausages fried, a lamb chop, toast.

The sound of a wireless coming faintly through glass, the fondness of the windows along the shore, the smell of wood fires are magnetic. If you never had a compass or a sounding-lead or a chart, they would draw you safely in.

The moorings lap and shift, water slapping on the clinker hulls. The slip is wet in the ebb – in the dark, easy to lose your balance. There is an iron ring near the top to make the painter fast. The poetry of cold, forbidding places.

He woke from a pleasant dream and saw his sister standing at the water's edge looking quizzically at him. He smiled and gestured to her to sit beside him. She may have been bathing: she had on that loose dress she usually wore afterwards. She did not move.

Even you, he thought. *I trusted you.*

Then he saw that the woman was a stranger and that he was sitting on a beach in Italy and that he was alone again. Still, there was something familiar about her. She was coming towards him now.

'What did you say?' she said.

He could not remember. But her accent was clear enough.

'You're Irish,' he said. He was pleased.

'And you?' she said. She meant: 'Has Oxford changed you?' The answer was, of course, too complex. And, anyway, it was too soon to tell after one term. David stood behind. They had met before, when she came up to visit, and so she was not formal. She smiled at him.

'Are you all right?'

He indicated the chair again, and this time she sat down. His father stepped from the boat at that moment and held up seven silver mackerel in greeting, their backs curved as though they had been hooked in the very instant of turning aside. They had left their getaway too late. He was smiling. 'Have them for tea, why don't you,' he said. 'We all will. They're the first of the season.'

'Father, this is David, my friend.' He was irritated by his inability to avoid inflecting the word. 'You remember I wrote to you that he might come down?'

His father turned away to tie the boat off.

His sister made an awkward joke, and for a few moments they discussed the scenery, the beautiful weather, how he had come down. His father put the mackerel into a canvas bag and picked up his rod. It seemed as if he looked at David only then.

'Do you people eat fish?' he asked, gazing steadfastly at him. David did not reply; he was sensitive to such things. His father watched him for a moment, something like amusement in his eyes, and then said, almost under his breath, 'They do resent things, don't they?'

And this was after they had heard the news from Europe. His father never changed. If he was constant in all things, stern